THE BEVERLY GRAY

MYSTERY STORIES

# BEVERLY GRAY'S ADVENTURE

"IN THE WRONG HANDS YOUR INVENTION COULD WRECK THE WORLD," BEVERLY SAID, AGHAST.

*Beverly Gray's Adventure*

# BEVERLY GRAY'S
# ADVENTURE

## By CLAIR BLANK

GROSSET & DUNLAP

*Publishers*      New York

# Contents

# BEVERLY GRAY'S ADVENTURE

## CHAPTER I

# Failure

---

"BEVERLY!" Lenora raced up the stairs, disturbing the peaceful quiet which usually hung over the house. "Beverly!" she repeated, bursting into the room where three other girls were busy sewing or reading.

"What is it?" Lois Mason inquired, looking up in surprise.

"Beverly, get your hat," Lenora cried. "We have an assignment."

"Oh, for the life of a newspaper girl!" Shirley Parker sighed. "If you don't stop rushing around—"

"I like it!" Lenora declared. "It makes me feel important," she beamed.

"Where are we to go?" Beverly Gray inquired, slipping into her coat.

"Long Island. There has been an explosion."

"Take my car," Shirley offered at once.

The girls departed in a rush. They got Shirley's car from the garage across the street and, with Beverly at the wheel, headed for Long Island. Mr. Blaine had given Lenora only meager directions as to how to reach the spot, but they need not have worried. They found dozens of cars moving in the same direction. Traffic was slow. Impatient drivers sounded horns. A police siren wailed through the darkness. Once they had to pull off the narrow road entirely to let a fire engine roar past.

A car pulled up beside them and Katharine Merrill, reporter for the *Sun* and the girls' rival, stuck her head out an open window.

"Hi, there! What's going on?"

"You can read about it in the *Tribune* tomorrow," Lenora answered generously.

Katharine made a wry face at her and looked at Beverly. "What do you know?"

"I thought you were on your way to Florida," Lenora interrupted before Beverly could answer.

"Next month," Katharine returned, and disappeared as the cars pulled apart.

"What did Mr. Blaine tell you about the explosion?" Beverly asked.

"Just that it is the house of Kurt Kresloff, the inventor," Lenora replied. "But don't ask me what he invents."

Beverly had no opportunity to comment. They turned from the main highway into a private drive that wound between two high stone walls. Ordinarily trespassers were barred from the estate by a high iron gate, but today the gate stood ajar and vehicles of all descriptions streamed into the estate.

"Everybody in town must have heard about it," Lenora commented.

The house was a massive brownstone edifice surrounded by shrubs and flowers. About a hundred yards from the house was another stone building. It was in this that the explosion had occurred. There was a huge gaping black hole in one wall and smoke still hung in a haze about the roof. There were no windows, but at the moment the door hung brokenly on one hinge and police kept spectators from crowding into the building.

A fine, stinging rain had started and as the girls climbed out of the parked car, they ran for the protection of the trees. Katharine Merrill joined them as they approached the police guarding the wrecked building.

Their press cards gained them admittance to the building, but what there was to see had to be seen with the aid of flashlights. The electrical system had been damaged in the explosion. The flashlights revealed that the building had been used as a laboratory, but now it was merely a mass of broken glass and apparatus. As yet the police had not succeeded in discovering the cause of the explosion. The inventor had not been in the laboratory at the time and he could offer no explanation.

"There is nothing to be seen here," Lenora sighed. "Let's find Mr. Kresloff."

They left the laboratory to the police and curious spectators and walked to the house. Police were stationed at the door here, too, and they informed the girls that the inventor would speak to no one.

"We just want some information on the explosion," Beverly said.

"Mr. Kresloff doesn't want any publicity," the officer told them firmly. "He won't speak to any reporters."

"He is a famous man. The public is interested in what happens to him," Katharine Merrill insisted.

"Mr. Kresloff isn't interested in the public," was the retort. "You might as well go home, girls."

"I can't go home," Lenora told Beverly as they moved away from the house. "Charlie Blaine expressly told me to get a picture of Kurt Kresloff. I can't go back without it. He'll be sorry he gave me a job."

Katharine Merrill shook her head. "Haven't you heard? They call Kresloff 'The Man Who Hates Cameras.' There is no existing picture of him that we have been able to find. He hides from photographers."

"Why?"

"No one knows." Katharine pulled her coat closer. "I guess I'll go back to the laboratory and see what kind of a story I can get out of the wreck."

"I'll go with you," Beverly said. "Coming, Lenora?"

"No." The other girl shook her head. "I think I'll wander around the grounds."

"Good hunting!" Katharine Merrill called.

Lenora watched the other girls disappear in the rain and then she turned back toward the house. Lights blazed from all the windows. Police went in and out constantly.

It was hopeless to think of slipping inside that way, yet slip inside she must if she hoped to get a picture of the inventor. She left the main drive and followed a small flagstone path around a corner of the house. French windows opened off the terrace and Lenora thought how simple it would be to enter through them. One window stood invitingly ajar. Heavy curtains hung across the windows, protecting the room from curious eyes, but a crack of light was visible where the two curtains came together, and it seemed to beckon to her like a finger.

Noiselessly Lenora stepped inside. Standing between the curtains and the windows, she listened intently for both a sound outside that would indicate someone had seen her and was following, and a sound inside that would tell her if someone occupied the room. Nothing but the beating of the rain on the windows came to her.

Through the parting of the curtains she could see a large, low-ceilinged room—a library, and unoccupied. She was about to step forward when she heard voices and the door opened. Two men stepped into the room. One man sat down at a desk and in a moment the other went out. Lenora wondered if the man at the desk was the inventor. It must be, for he seemed perfectly at home.

She took her camera from its case, made sure the flash unit was ready, and stepped out from behind the curtains. She focused the camera on the man at the desk, called "Mr. Kresloff!" and snapped the picture just as he looked directly at her.

It was Lenora's thought to escape immediately with her prize, but before the curtains dropped behind her a hand closed on her arm.

"Give me that camera!" The inventor's voice was cold with anger as he towered over her.

"I'm a newspaper photographer," Lenora explained hastily. "We are doing a story on the explosion—"

"The camera, please!" He reached out and took it from her. He extracted the plate and smashed it on the desk. Then he handed the camera back to Lenora.

"Now leave the grounds before I have the police arrest you for trespassing," he ordered.

Lenora left in undignified haste and as she emerged onto the terrace, she bumped into Beverly.

"I've been looking for you," Beverly said. "Are you ready to leave?"

"It is a shame the explosion missed him!" Lenora burst out. "Of all the ill-mannered—"

"Whoa!" Beverly laughed. "What are you talking about?"

Lenora proceeded to pour out the story of what had happened.

"What will Charlie Blaine say?" she finished gloomily. "Mr. Kresloff refuses to have his picture taken!"

"Mr. Blaine will understand and probably give you another chance. If what Katharine Merrill said is true, no one else succeeded either."

"But I will," Lenora promised. "I'm coming back to see Mr. Kresloff some day soon. I'll haunt the place until I get a picture. Nobody can break my camera plates and get away with it!"

## CHAPTER II

## *Assignment*

---

As THE girls were leaving the office, having made their report on the explosion, Charlie Blaine called Beverly back for a moment.

"Be here at nine o'clock tomorrow morning—alone," he directed. "Without Lenora."

"Very well," Beverly agreed, puzzled.

She joined Lenora and they stopped at Smitty's for their dinner. Then they returned Shirley's car to the garage and went home.

Beverly was in the *Tribune* office at the appointed time the following morning. She had left Lenora eating her breakfast, but she knew the blond girl would follow as soon as possible. There was a tall, thin man with Charlie

Blaine when Beverly entered the latter's office, and she recognized him as Lieutenant Petersen, of the Intelligence Department, whom she had met before. After the first greetings were over, Charlie Blaine explained the officer's presence.

"The Lieutenant has a big story for us, Beverly. He wants you—"

"Suppose you let me tell Miss Gray," Lieutenant Petersen smiled. "You helped us once before, when we were after the Ghost Club, and that is why I am calling on you again."

Beverly remained silent, wondering what was coming.

"Of course, you are privileged to say 'no' to the whole affair," the Lieutenant smiled. "It is purely voluntary. I want you to understand that. You can hear what I have to say and then decide, but whether you accept or not, what is said here is confidential."

"Yes, sir," Beverly murmured.

Lieutenant Petersen sat down in a chair next to hers and began his story.

"We have reason to believe that a man, well-known and apparently a good citizen, is working against our Government. Our attempts to secure definite information about him, or to determine exactly what he is working on, have failed. He is smart and has been able to recognize all the secret service operators we put on his trail. We know he is a definite threat to the safety of our country, but we can't prove it. What we need is someone, not connected in any way with our department, who is willing to try to discover what he is planning, who his accomplices are, where he gets his money—everything it is possible to know."

"That is a large order," Beverly smiled.

The Lieutenant nodded. "The man is very difficult to approach. He won't talk to the press at all. He doesn't go in for much social life, and there are few people that he trusts. You will be doing your country a great service," Lieutenant Petersen continued gravely, "but you must not underestimate the risk involved. There is danger. We have no idea what he is doing, so we do not know what to warn you against. All we can say is that even though he seems harmless on the surface, he is not."

"How would I become acquainted with him?" Beverly asked.

"He is looking for a secretary. He has made inquiries of some of his friends. You will take the position."

"It means giving up the *Tribune* for a while," Charlie Blaine added. "You must be connected in no way with the paper. Even Lenora must not know what you are doing."

"But Lenora would never believe that I quit the paper!" Beverly exclaimed. "We were to work together on a series of articles in competition with Katharine Merrill's cross-country series, have you forgotten?"

"You must make your friend believe you have quit," Lieutenant Petersen said firmly. "From the moment you take this assignment your life must be different. You must not confide in anyone. Too much depends upon the secrecy with which you handle the job."

"It will not be easy—" Beverly began.

"No," the officer agreed. "It will be most difficult."

There was a moment of silence as both he and Charlie Blaine looked expectantly at the girl before them.

"Well?" Charlie Blaine said at last.

"I'll try," Beverly answered. "Who is the man?"

An hour later Beverly walked up Broadway lost in thought. Kurt Kresloff! The name still echoed in her ears. The man who refused to see or have anything to do with the press. The man who would not permit his picture to be taken. The man who had no windows in his laboratory and who refused to explain mysterious explosions there. Quite suddenly he and his strange ideas had become her problem. On her shoulders had descended the most important assignment of her career, the biggest adventure of her life.

Lieutenant Petersen had supplied her with names and addresses of people she could use as references. If Kresloff investigated, they would give her such high recommendations that there would be small chance of her failing to get the position as his secretary. Now she went home to write the letter of application which Lieutenant Petersen had suggested.

When she reached the apartment she found Shirley in the process of dressing for her matinee performance and Lenora and Lois absent. She wrote her letter, had lunch with Shirley, and went for a long walk in the park. When she returned, Lois and Lenora were preparing dinner.

"What happened to you?" Lenora demanded. "Did you go out on a story without me?"

Beverly laughed and evaded the question. "Are you feeling well? Since when have you become interested in domestic duties?"

"She wants to impress Terry with her cooking the next time he pops in, so she is practicing on us," Lois laughed.

Lenora flicked a few drops of water in her friend's face and dodged as Lois retaliated.

"I hope nothing ever happens to change us," Lenora sighed happily.

"Change us?" Beverly asked. "Why do you say that?"

"We get along so well," Lenora explained. "We have no secrets from each other, we never quarrel—"

Lois nodded in agreement. "Heaven sends us our relatives but we choose our friends, and the Alpha Deltas have chosen each other. Why should we quarrel? After all this time together it would take an earthquake to separate us."

"An earthquake!" Lenora echoed vigorously.

Beverly, watching them, remembered Lieutenant Petersen's instructions that she must not confide in anyone. She would have a secret from them, and it made her wonder if she were to provide the earthquake that would destroy their friendship. What would happen when they began asking questions she must not answer?

The four girls were at breakfast the next morning when the telephone rang. Beverly answered it and was immediately alert.

"Miss Gray?"

"Yes."

"Are you the Miss Gray who wrote a letter requesting an interview for a position with Mr. Kurt Kresloff?" asked the voice at the other end of the wire.

"Yes," Beverly said again, almost holding her breath in anticipation.

"Mr. Kresloff will interview you. Will two o'clock this afternoon be convenient?"

"Yes, it would," Beverly replied instantly, her heart beating fast.

"We will expect you at two, then," the cool voice went on. "Do you know where Mr. Kresloff's estate is located?"

"Yes," Beverly replied. "I will be there at two o'clock."

Beverly dressed carefully and took a bus out to Long Island, timing her arrival to the minute. The watchman at the high iron gate of the estate let her in and personally conducted her to the house where he turned her over to a tall, stern-faced butler. The latter led her to a small reception room and asked her to wait.

The interview was even more strenuous than Beverly had anticipated. She talked first to a gray-haired man who said he was representing Mr. Kresloff. After she answered his questions, satisfactorily she hoped, he made a telephone call and then ushered her into another room. The walls were lined with books and the rug was deep and soft, deadening all sound. Curtains were drawn over the windows, making the light dim and mellow. A man sat behind a huge desk, his hands folded on a pile of papers, watching her as she walked toward him. Instinctively she knew this was Kurt Kresloff.

Then there were more questions, more searching inquiries, and more studied answers. She was doing as Lieutenant Petersen had instructed her, saying the words he had given her, and she could only hope she was being believed.

"Miss Gray, what I need is someone who is willing to spend long hours in research and in typing notes of my experiments. The hours are unusual and uncertain, but the salary and working conditions are excellent. I have already contacted the people to whom you referred me, and you are more highly recommended than any of the other applicants.

"The work is confidential and though sometimes it may seem to you to be of little consequence, I assure you it is all important. The smallest error might destroy months of work. I want someone who is accurate, someone who will do what she is told and not ask questions. If you believe you can handle it, the position is yours."

"When shall I start?" Beverly asked quietly.

"Tomorrow." The inventor looked at his watch and rose. "If you like, I will show you where you are to work and then we can start as soon as you arrive in the morning."

He led the way upstairs to a room at the front of the house. A desk, typewriter stand, telephone, two chairs, and a filing cabinet had been moved into the room which, at one time, had been a bedroom.

"This is your office," he smiled. "The windows overlook the best part of the garden and catch any breeze there is. If there is anything you want at any time, just push the button on your desk and Forrest, the butler, will get it for you. As I said, you will type my notes and letters and take care of my telephone calls. You will find a lot of the work will have to do with the charities in which I am interested, but I don't believe there will be anything very difficult."

Later, as she walked down the driveway on her way out, Beverly had the uncomfortable feeling that eyes were watching her from the house. Then, at last, she was out on the road, with the high gate shut behind her. She took a deep breath and shut her eyes just for a minute. Her hands were ice cold and her heart was beating like a trip hammer, but over it all came a glow of triumph. The first hurdle was taken. Tomorrow she would start her duties here. She would not go to the *Tribune* office with Lenora. Instead she would come out to Beechwood. The gate would open for her and she would enter upon a new and strange world.

## CHAPTER III

## *Deception*

---

"I'M GIVING up my job on the *Tribune,*" Beverly announced the next morning at the breakfast table.

Lenora dropped her glass of orange juice and the other girls stared in startled amazement.

Beverly handed Lenora a napkin and repeated her statement. This was going to be harder than she had thought. The girls knew her too well. They knew what her job on the newspaper meant to her.

"Oh," Lois said, clearing her throat. "You are getting married. I always knew we'd lose you, but—"

Beverly shook her head. "No, not yet. I'm taking another job."

"Doing what?" Shirley asked.

"Doing some typing and research work for a scientist," Beverly explained. "It is a chance to use the chemistry I studied in college."

All this while Lenora said nothing. She sat and stared at Beverly. At last she shook her head. "I don't understand, Bev. The paper—your job reporting—they always came first with you. Now you are quitting. Just like that—" she snapped her fingers. "Why?"

Beverly shrugged her shoulders, keeping her voice deliberately low and steady as she spoke.

"I just feel I want to change, that's all."

"It isn't like you to give up the newspaper," Lenora persisted.

"I'm doing it," Beverly stated and, leaving the table, picked up her handbag and hat and went out quickly.

Beverly took the bus to Long Island, as she had done the previous day. The procedure was the same, too. The gateman let her in and led the way up to the house. The butler took her coat and led her to the library. There, on the threshold of the massive room, she hesitated. One more step and it would be too late to go back. It was too late already, she told herself, and entered the room, her head high.

"Good morning, Miss Gray."

She jumped as the inventor came out of the shadows by the far wall of books.

"I'm glad you are early," he said. "I don't often quote the adage about the early birds, but I like early birds nevertheless. I'll take you upstairs to your room and you can get right to work."

He followed Beverly out into the hall, talking pleasantly as they mounted the stairs.

"The very nature of this position, Miss Gray, makes it almost impossible for you to have regular hours. Quite possibly I shall keep you late one night and not need you at all the next day. However, I am sure things will adjust themselves rapidly. You won't find me a hard taskmaster. You probably will have a lot of free time. Forrest the butler will serve you your lunch in your office. Do you have a car?" he asked presently.

"I have been thinking of getting one," Beverly answered.

"It would be a valuable asset because I shall quite often have to send you in to town. Of course, when my own car is not in use you may drive that. You do drive, don't you?"

"Oh, yes," Beverly said.

"Good!" He opened the door to the room she had seen yesterday and stood aside. "I'm sure you will find everything you need. If not, Forrest will get it for you." He picked up a portfolio of papers from the desk. "These are some notes I have made the past week on experiments I have been conducting. Your knowledge of chemistry will help you in typing them. Now I'll leave and you can get right to work."

He was gone in an instant, leaving Beverly staring at her surroundings. When the door was closed she felt completely cut off from the rest of the house. The rug deadened her footsteps as she walked to the window and flung it wide. A timid ray of sunshine fell across one corner of the desk and it seemed like a friendly hand as she sat down and endeavored to feel at ease.

The morning went swiftly. It seemed she had barely started typing when there was a discreet knock at the door and the butler brought in a delicious luncheon on a tray. Beverly tried to talk to him but he replied in monosyllables and it was plain that he did not care to hold a conversation with her.

In mid-afternoon she finished typing all the notes and put them in a neat pile. Then she ventured downstairs to the library. It was empty, but upon emerging into the hall again, she bumped into the butler.

"Do you know where Mr. Kresloff is?"

"He has gone out, Miss. If you are finished typing, he said you might go home."

Beverly nodded and went back upstairs. She got her hat and took the notes down to the inventor's desk in the library. Then she went out and down the driveway. Her first day was over and what had she learned? That Mr. Kresloff had a neat, precise handwriting, that his notes were minute and many, and that his house was quiet almost to the point of being oppressive. There had been nothing to indicate he was not what he seemed to be. She sighed as she walked to the bus stop. She was not sure what she had expected to learn in one day. It would be harder than she had anticipated to find anything amiss in his affairs.

Larry was still working at the Long Island plant of the airplane company and now, instead of going back to town, she went to his office. She rarely bothered him during business hours, but she had not seen him for three days and now she wanted him to help her buy an automobile.

"You may use my car," Larry said generously when Beverly told him her intentions. "You don't have to buy one."

"Then what will you do?" she asked. "Besides, I want a shiny, new one."

"Okay," he laughed. "I'll help you spend the proceeds from your play."

Larry took her to a friend of his who was happy to demonstrate the car she had in mind. In scarcely any time at all, she found herself the owner of a sleek, powerful roadster which would be delivered to her within the next day or so.

Beverly and Larry dined downtown and afterward went to a concert. Sitting in the darkness, listening to the swelling rapture of the music, her hand held tightly and warmly in his, Beverly almost forgot Kurt Kresloff and the double role she must play. She wished suddenly that she could discuss it with Larry. He was always an excellent confidant, ready with comfort, advice, encouragement—whatever she needed most. When the music ended to thunderous applause, Beverly and Larry made their way up the aisle and slowly home to Mrs. Callahan's.

The girls all were in bed when Beverly entered. Noiselessly she undressed and crawled in beside Shirley. She was glad no one was awake to ask questions about her announcement of that morning.

Beverly was up and gone before the others had breakfast the following morning. By not giving them an opportunity to ask questions, she could avoid having to tell lies or deceive them. She could not tell them what she was doing, so the simplest thing was not to tell them anything.

She was able to avoid the issue until Sunday when Lenora woke her.

"Beverly, my cherub!" Lenora bounced on Beverly's bed and sat cross-legged at the foot. "Want to go on a picnic with us?"

Beverly opened one eye, viewed her friend, and closed it again.

"No, thanks."

"Why not?"

"I have something else to do." It was the truth. Kresloff had asked her to work for a short while that morning.

"Skip it," Lenora said promptly. "We don't have a picnic every day. The whole gang is going."

"Sorry," Beverly said. "I hope you have a good time."

"We want you there, too," Lenora persisted.

"I really can't make it," Beverly said, turning over to bury her face in the pillow.

Lenora sat in thoughtful silence for a moment. "Okay," she said and then got up and went out, while Beverly sat up to stare at the door as it closed after her friend.

Lenora took her place at the breakfast table and silently sipped her orange juice while Shirley and Lois chattered brightly.

"It's a lovely day for a picnic," Lois sighed. "Don't you think so, Lenora?"

Silence greeted her remark.

"Lenora!"

"Huh? What did you say?"

"I don't believe you are awake yet," Lois laughed.

"I was thinking," Lenora informed her loftily. "What do you suppose is the matter with Beverly?"

"Is she sick?" Shirley asked at once.

Lenora shook her head. "I mean—she is acting so strangely. I asked her to come on the picnic and she said 'No, thanks' as cool as you please."

"Maybe she just doesn't like picnics," Lois shrugged.

"I don't much myself. It's the bugs that get me—"

"It isn't only the picnic," Lenora shook her head. "There is something else. Haven't you noticed it?"

"I have," Shirley volunteered.

"She is in love, or have you forgotten?" Lois murmured. "I believe that is supposed to make one a little dreamy and forgetful of other people. Ah, love!" She sighed and the other girls giggled.

"You sound like an ad for the marriage license bureau," Lenora commented. "Let's do the dishes and get ready."

Beverly got up and dressed in silence. Without even going into the kitchen where the other girls were, she left the apartment and stopped in Smitty's to have her breakfast.

Smitty, who had served them meals on various occasions for quite a while now, greeted her with a smile.

"Alone?" Her question was both a criticism and a probe for information.

"Yes," Beverly said calmly.

"This is the third morning this week you've come in alone for breakfast. Aren't your friends home?" Smitty inquired with friendly curiosity.

"Yes, they are home," Beverly stated and turned her attention to the menu, hoping Smitty would take the gesture as one of dismissal.

"Oh," said Smitty and walked away.

"Why should she care?" Beverly asked herself angrily. A second later her anger died and she knew Smitty had only meant to be friendly. "Careful, Beverly," she warned herself. She must not let things get on her nerves. This game had a long way to run and she had a foreboding that before she was through she would need all the patience, all the tact, and all the courage she could muster. Working in the dark—not having anyone to confide in or discuss problems with—would be the most difficult part.

There was not much for her to do at Beechwood, only a few notes to be typed, one or two telephone calls to make, and then Kresloff departed for Washington. He would be back late tomorrow afternoon, but until then her time was her own. She went back to the apartment, empty now that the girls had gone on their picnic, and sat a while at her typewriter, trying to write the beginning of another book. But the words would not come, so she went out for a walk in the park.

She ate a solitary dinner and went home to write letters.

She was in bed and pretended to be asleep when the other girls wearily stumbled in, and she rose the next morning before anyone else was awake.

Kresloff seemed to be in very good humor when he returned from Washington. Beverly wondered what his business had been and whether it had anything to do with her being at Beechwood. She already had carefully gone over the papers in the file in her room and found nothing significant. Kresloff seemed to do a great deal of charity work, lending both his house and his time to raising money for various causes.

Day after day Beverly went to Beechwood. After her car was delivered the trip was much easier, for she no longer had to go and come on a bus schedule. However, things at the apartment were not easy. She knew she could not expect the girls to accept her change of occupation calmly. Lenora, especially, was mystified. She waited for Beverly one evening and though it was late and the others were in bed, she took Beverly into the kitchen, sat on the edge of the table, and over crossed arms frowned at her friend.

"Beverly Gray, are you going to tell me what this is all about? When you said you were leaving the *Tribune* I thought you were joking. Then I realized you meant it, but I still thought you would be back within a week. What are you doing? Where do you go every day? What kind of a job do you have? Please explain!"

"There is nothing to explain," Beverly said, getting herself a drink of water. "I just got another job."

"Is that all you are going to say?" Lenora asked in a quiet voice.

Beverly realized that this moment was important. In those few words Lenora was reminding her of their friendship, the confidences they always shared, everything they had ever done together. Lenora was reminding her and asking to be let in on this new thing.

"That's all," Beverly nodded, not meeting her friend's eyes.

Lenora got to her feet and quietly and slowly walked out of the room. For a second Beverly could not move. It was as though her world was turning suddenly black all around her. She knew that from now on Lenora would ask no more questions. Nor would the other girls ask questions, for Lenora would tell them Beverly had rebuffed her.

No matter how important this assignment was, Beverly thought furiously, it could not be worth the loss of a friend. She started after Lenora but it was as though an invisible hand stayed her. She had given her solemn word to Lieutenant Petersen that she would tell no one what she was doing. The only comfort she could hold to was the thought that when it was all over she could explain to Lenora and be forgiven.

## CHAPTER IV

## *Suspicion*

BEVERLY was very careful at her work. She kept her eyes and ears open, but she could discover nothing worth while. The only one who troubled her was the butler. She did not trust him. His movements were noiseless on the thick rugs and she was forever coming upon him around corners or at closed doors. He never said a word when he was thus discovered, merely bowed to her and went on his silent way. Perhaps Lieutenant Petersen was mistaken in his suspicion of Kurt Kresloff. Perhaps it was the butler who was behind anything mysterious there might be at Beechwood.

One morning Kresloff came into her office with the request:

"Miss Gray, will you please type this note and deliver it in person to the people on this list? Then you may take the rest of the day off. I shall be busy in my laboratory and I won't need you again until tomorrow."

"Yes, sir," she said.

Beverly typed the short note he gave her and enclosed each copy in an envelope addressed to the individual to whom it was to go. Then she put on her hat and left to deliver each one personally.

When she had delivered the five notes, she still had the afternoon before her. What to do? It was becoming more and more difficult to go back to the apartment and face the girls. She could see the speculation and unasked questions in their eyes when she had to refuse an invitation to join in their fun and go out alone on some mysterious errand. They did not understand and she could not explain. She had to ignore their hurt silence and it was not easy. The Alpha Deltas always had been frank with each other. It was not that she, personally, did not trust them. It was Lieutenant Petersen who did not, and he had imposed that restriction upon her.

She drove past the theater where *Angels Arise* was playing and upon impulse went in. The play would soon close for the summer season. This might be her last chance to see it, and, besides, the theater would be an ideal place to pass a few hours. Once more she could watch Shirley give life to the character which she, Beverly, had created on her typewriter.

Beverly looked at Shirley's picture on the billboard in front of the theater and realized again how much the success of the play had depended upon her friend. Shirley had stepped into the part at the last moment and carried the play to glorious success. Her portrayal of the leading character was the result of long discussions with Beverly. They had carefully gone over every scene, every gesture, until Shirley knew perfectly what Beverly had had in mind when she wrote the play. It had enabled her to give a flawless performance. The success of *Angels Arise* had been like a dream come true—the dream they had shared in college that some day Beverly would write a play and Shirley would star in it.

The fact that people should praise her for words she had written never failed to make Beverly feel proud and yet humble. It was a treasure within her, that gift for portraying scenes and people with words. It was like a flame that must be cherished and guarded.

"How do you do it, Beverly? Where do you get your ideas?" One of the Alpha Delta girls had asked her that the day after her play opened.

"I don't know," she had replied laughingly.

It was true. She did not know where the ideas or the words came from. They formed in her mind and flowed out through her fingertips onto the typewriter keys. All she had done was try to make other people see a tiny corner of the world as she had seen it. That they had liked it was at once both gratifying and amazing to her.

When the play was over she went out with the crowd. Always before, she had gone backstage to compliment Shirley on her performance, but not today. She went out to her car and found a young man leaning against the fender, waiting for her.

"Larry! What a nice surprise!" she exclaimed.

"I hope you think so," he said, taking her arm. "Come along, I want to talk to you."

She looked up smilingly, expecting to see a teasing glint in his eyes, but his face was grave, almost stern.

Larry led the way to a small restaurant where odors of

cooking gave promise of a delicious dinner and where checkered cloths and shaded lights gave an air of pleasant friendliness. They chose a table under an imitation tree and Larry ordered for both of them. When the waiter had gone away, Larry looked at her with a frown.

"Why didn't you tell me you had quit the newspaper?"

Beverly took a deep breath to steady herself. This, then, was the cause of that sober expression on his face.

"I intended to," she said, "but we've both been so busy—"

"What are you doing?" he asked.

"Typing and research work. I'm a secretary," she announced. "It is nice to have my own office, no more running around at all hours, rushing to make a dead line—" even to her own ears her words sounded flat and false.

Larry simply stared at her. "Bev—I don't understand. You always said the only time you would leave the paper was when we got married. Now—"

"I know," she said unhappily. She touched his hand almost timidly. "Are you angry, Larry?"

"No," he said slowly, "just puzzled. Tell me about your job. Where is it? For whom do you work?"

At that moment the waiter brought their dinner and

created a timely interruption. Beverly praised the tasty meal and brought up the subject of her next book. She discussed the plot with Larry, carefully keeping the conversation away from her new job, and when she left him much later he still had no definite information about what she was doing. But she was troubled and unhappy. It was not her nature to be misleading and secretive, and she would be happy indeed when the whole affair was closed.

The following day when Beverly finished her morning's work, she gathered up the notes and started down the stairs to go to the laboratory to see if Kresloff had anything more for her to do.

"I'd like to see Mr. Kresloff," a voice stated clearly and firmly at the door below.

It was a familiar voice, but Beverly did not realize it at first. When she did, it was too late to draw back out of sight. Katharine Merrill stood in the hall, facing the butler, demanding to see the inventor. How she had gotten inside the high iron gate Beverly could not guess.

Katharine's eyes widened in surprise when she saw Beverly, and she opened her lips to speak. But Beverly did not betray her recognition of the other girl by the faintest smile or glance. She walked swiftly past without turning her head and closed the front door behind her, giving the *Sun* reporter no chance to speak to her.

Beverly went immediately to the laboratory and gave Mr. Kresloff the typed notes. He was hard at work and merely glanced over his shoulder at her.

"There are some figures to be typed also," he said. "Please take them."

At that moment there was a knock on the door and the butler came in.

"What do you want, Forrest?"

"There is a young lady to see you—a reporter."

"I never talk to reporters," the inventor said. "You know that."

"Yes, sir, I told her that, but she refuses to go away without speaking to you. She says she has only one question to ask you."

"I never talk to reporters," the inventor repeated, never looking up from his work.

"Don't you want to hear my one question?"

Katharine Merrill stood in the doorway. She had followed the butler and boldly stepped inside while they were discussing her. From her position in the corner of the room, half-hidden by a row of test tubes, Beverly watched the inventor slowly straighten and face the reporter.

"I will listen to your question," he said wearily. "But I do not promise to answer it."

"Are you the same Kurt Kresloff who had to leave England because of your anti-British activities?"

"I have heard your question, now will you please leave?" The inventor turned his back on the girl and resumed his work.

Katharine Merrill shrugged her shoulders and went out. The butler followed silently. Beverly gathered up her notes, covertly watching Kresloff, but there was nothing to indicate that he was in any way disturbed.

Beverly typed the figures he had given her, left them on his desk, and got her coat to go home. When she emerged into the garden the sun had surrendered the world to cool, purple twilight. She got into her car, waved farewell to the man at the gate, and sped along the narrow road. As she came round a bend about a mile from Beechwood, a slender figure stepped into the path of her car and Beverly jammed on the brake. Katharine Merrill opened the door and climbed in beside her.

"I waited for you," she explained unnecessarily.

Beverly cast a hasty glance into the rear-vision mirror to be sure no one was following.

"Come on, confess all," the new passenger commanded.

Beverly laughed. "I'm his secretary, that's all."

"That's all!" Katharine exclaimed. "That is only the beginning. You couldn't give up reporting any more than I could. You might as well tell me what it is all about."

"There is nothing to tell," Beverly said. "What did you mean by the question you asked him?"

"I have information to the effect that Kurt Kresloff was accused by Scotland Yard of selling secret formulas for explosives to foreign powers and plotting against the Government. I had the idea he might be doing the same thing here—what with the explosions he has been having."

Beverly was silent, wondering. Was this what Lieutenant Petersen suspected, too?

"What is it all about?" Katharine watched the other girl closely. "I knew the minute I saw you that something was up."

"I'm acting as his secretary," Beverly replied. "He doesn't know I was ever a reporter. If he had known, I might not have gotten the job. He doesn't like reporters," she added.

"You're telling me!" was the retort. "But you don't expect me to believe you have really left the *Tribune,* do you?"

"What does it look like?" Beverly evaded.

"If it is your story, I'll stay off it," Katharine promised, "but satisfy my curiosity. Is he a dangerous man?"

"He has been very nice to me," Beverly replied.

"That tells me a lot!"

"There is nothing to tell," Beverly repeated, expertly guiding the car through a maze of traffic.

The other girl was silent for a moment.

"Okay, be a Sphinx if you want to."

Beverly longed to ask her if she contemplated doing anything more about Kresloff, but she did not dare. It would bring forth a lot of questions that she herself could not answer. It was better to let Katharine think whatever she wanted.

## CHAPTER V

## *Developments*

---

ONE day, shortly after his return from Washington, Kresloff told Beverly he was lending his estate to the Foster Children's Home for a garden party. All the money gained from admission fees, luncheon, souvenirs, etc., would be turned over to the Home. Beverly felt it was very generous of him to turn his house and grounds into a show place for charity, especially since he valued his privacy, and she eagerly helped with plans. It kept her busy and for that she was glad. Perhaps at the garden party she might learn something worth while—something to report to Lieutenant Petersen.

The afternoon of the affair was a gloriously sunny, not-too-warm day and people began arriving at an early hour. Gay beach umbrellas shaded the luncheon tables. A striped tent had been erected close to the garage and in this a fortuneteller held audience.

Beverly wandered about among the guests, looking she did not know for what. She felt this afternoon was important, yet she did not know why. What could there be suspicious about a garden party given for charity?

Then Beverly saw her. At first glance she scarcely recognized the smiling woman lunching with Kresloff, but after a second glance, a warning note sounded somewhere within her and she looked more carefully. Was it possible after all this time, or was the sunlight playing tricks on her eyes? The Countess! Beverly was sure it was she, and yet—

It had been quite a while since the Countess disappeared after the capture of the Ghost Club. Beverly had had a glimpse of her in Cuba not so long ago, but to find her here was a shock. The police were still searching for the elusive member of the Ghost Club and here she sat— openly enjoying herself for all to see. That was what made it so hard to believe—that this really was the

Countess, that she would be so bold. Beverly knew she must make sure.

Beverly began moving closer and then she stopped, caught by the sudden realization that the Countess would recognize her, too. All Lieutenant Petersen's carefully laid plans would go for naught. The Countess knew Beverly as a reporter and she would most certainly tell Kresloff. Beverly withdrew behind the fortuneteller's tent to consider the matter.

"Is something wrong, Miss?" Forrest was at her elbow with his deferential bow.

"Do you know the woman talking to Mr. Kresloff?" Beverly asked impulsively.

"I believe she is an old friend of Mr. Kresloff," Forrest replied, giving her a sharp glance. "Do you know her?"

"I'm not sure," Beverly murmured. "What is her name?"

"Mrs. Dwight Portage."

"Does she live in New York?" Beverly continued.

"Yes, Miss. Why don't you ask Mr. Kresloff to introduce you?"

"In other words," Beverly thought wryly, "I shouldn't

ask so many questions. It isn't proper for the boss's secretary to gossip with the butler."

Mrs. Dwight Portage! Beverly watched the woman from a distance. Every gesture, every movement served to strengthen her suspicion. The Countess might change her name and dye her hair, but unless she could change every other characteristic, her identity would not be completely hidden.

Should she notify the authorities of what she suspected, or should she wait in the hope of learning why the Countess was so friendly with Kresloff? The Countess was usually involved in espionage and her very presence with Kresloff might be the clue for which Lieutenant Petersen was searching. Beverly decided to wait. If the Countess was such a good friend of Kresloff's, she would probably come to Beechwood again.

The garden party was a huge success, and Kresloff told Beverly later that a substantial sum of money had been realized. As the days passed Beverly began to worry about the fact that the Countess did not return to Beechwood. She began to regret that she had not sent word to Lieutenant Petersen about her. Then one day Kresloff wrote a letter to several people inviting them to a meeting at his house, and one of them was addressed to the Countess. Beverly felt a keen flash of interest when she thought of that meeting. It might lead to something interesting if she could see and hear what went on. However, the afternoon of the meeting, Kresloff came to her office and suggested that she take the rest of the day off.

"I still have some notes to type," Beverly said.

"Do them tomorrow."

"I haven't catalogued the research books yet," she continued.

"I think you should take the rest of the day off," he said quietly.

It was no longer a generous gesture. It was a command. He wanted her to leave Beechwood as much as she wanted to stay. There was nothing she could do but yield to his wishes. Whatever the meeting was about she was not destined to know.

Beverly got into her car and drove to the city. She had lunch and then strolled in the park. Over and over again she repeated to herself the words of the invitation about the meeting. There was nothing suspicious in it, yet the idea persisted in her mind that she was overlooking something.

Beverly found a vacant park bench and relaxed on it gratefully. If only there were someone she could talk to. She could not even talk to Larry! As if the mere thought of him had conjured him up beside her, she heard his voice.

"I have been sitting across from you staring at you for ten minutes," he laughed, "but you have been so busy thinking you didn't even see me."

"I'm sorry," she said, moving over a little to let him sit down beside her. "Why didn't you speak to me when I first sat down?"

"I guess I was thinking myself," he admitted, "because I wasn't aware of you until I thought of finding a telephone to call you."

"This is an odd hour for you to be sitting in the park," she declared. "Is anything wrong?"

"I had to meet one of the executives for lunch and then I decided to come here to consider my problem."

"What problem?" she asked.

"It will be your problem, too," he smiled. "You see, it is this way. The firm wants me to go to England, to their branch office there, and help them get started building our new model plane. It is a marvelous opportunity for me and will mean a lot to our future, Bev, but I'd be gone for several months," he said with a sidelong glance at her. "That is the part I don't like, unless—"

"Unless what?"

"Unless you will marry me now and go with me."

"Larry!" Her hand came out to him while she thought of the idea. There was no obstacle to their getting married—except Kurt Kresloff. Her job! She caught her breath sharply at the memory of how helpless she was. This thing, Lieutenant Petersen had said, was bigger than she was—bigger than all of them. She just could not drop everything and walk away. It would be an easy escape for her from the suspense and intrigue, but always the thought that she had run out on her biggest assignment would come back to haunt her.

"I can't, Larry," she said dully.

"Why not?" he rushed on eagerly. "We can be married and fly to England on the Clipper."

"I can't," she repeated through stiff lips. "I can't go now."

"Why not?"

"I can't explain," she said lamely.

Slowly she watched his eyes darken and the enthusiasm

fade from his face. His hands dropped from hers.

"I understand," he said. "It is asking you to give up a lot. Your mysterious job—your play—"

"It isn't that, Larry!" she cried. "I'd go with you in a minute! I want to more than anything, only—"

"Only you aren't quite sure," he murmured.

"I am sure," Beverly insisted. "I'd give anything, but—"

"Don't go on," Larry said stiffly. He stood up and gazed out across the pond where brown ducks were hunting for crumbs. "I have to go, of course, but not until next week. Suppose we have dinner together tomorrow night? There is a new play at the Liberty Theater—"

"Larry," she said softly. What she felt for Larry went deeper than words and now, as she said his name, her heart was in her eyes. When he looked at her, some of the hurt faded from his face. He bent and put his hands on her shoulders, holding her tightly.

"I want to believe that you have a good reason, Beverly, a reason there is no getting around. I will believe it. We'll have all our dreams some day, Bev."

"Of course," she whispered, and watched him walk away through a blur of tears. Then, with a sigh, she got up and went in the opposite direction to Mrs. Callahan's.

She was dressing for dinner when Shirley came in. As yet neither Lenora nor Lois were home.

"Well," Shirley sighed, "it won't be long before the show closes for the summer."

"No," Beverly agreed. "You've been marvelous in it."

Shirley sat down on the bed and watched Beverly comb her hair.

"Are you happy, Bev?" she asked abruptly.

For a moment Beverly's comb paused in mid-air as she replied: "Yes, why?"

"I've felt that during the past weeks you had something worrying you. Is there? Can I help?"

"No, thank you," Beverly said, her voice a little unsteady. "I'm sorry, Shirley, but I must run. Good-by."

Escape was all she could think of—escape from Shirley's keen eyes and humble gift of sincere friendship. It was too much, coming as it did, on top of her scene with Larry.

To Shirley, Beverly's hasty departure was a rebuff almost as strong as a slap in the face. She had been fairly burning with the desire to do anything to take them back to their old footing and Beverly had coolly said, "No, thank you." Shirley's gift of friendship and understanding had been ignored and after the first shock of surprise and hurt at Beverly's action, she began to grow angry. She was still warm with resentment when Lenora came in and wearily shoved her camera out of sight under the bed.

"If the phone rings, I am not home," Lenora announced. "Never again will I volunteer to take pictures of a parade! My feet are killing me!"

"Lenora, what are we going to do about Beverly?"

Lenora dropped on the bed and groaned. "Don't ask me riddles. I'm not up to them."

"Something must be done," Shirley declared.

"What?" Lenora wanted to know. "I've failed to think of anything we can do."

Shirley was silent. She, too, was at a loss as to what to do.

However, the next day events took an unexpected turn. Katharine Merrill telephoned Lenora and invited her to lunch.

"I thought you were to go on a tour and report interesting facts from different parts of the country," Lenora said suspiciously.

"I am," the *Sun* reporter assured her, "but there is something I must do first. Have lunch with me today?"

"Why?" Lenora asked frankly.

"Because I want to talk to you," was the laughing reply. "I'll meet you at the Drake at one o'clock."

Curious about what Katharine Merrill could have to say to her, Lenora made certain to be on time.

"Here I am," Lenora announced as she swept up to Katharine in the hotel lobby, her umbrella dripping all over the rug, and her breath coming in short gasps from hurrying through the rain. "Where do we eat?"

Katharine led the way to the dining room and the head waiter placed them at a small table in the corner.

"I thought we could eat here as well as talk."

"What about?" Lenora wanted to know. "I'm flattered, of course, that you asked me to lunch," she grinned, "but I feel you have an ulterior motive."

"I have," the other girl admitted. She smiled at Lenora. "You don't like me, do you?"

"Why should I?" Lenora inquired. "The way you ran out on Beverly and me at Vernon—"

"I'm sorry about that."

"Besides, we work on rival newspapers," Lenora added.

"I know, but I suggest that we call a truce for a while," Katharine proposed. "Do you agree?"

Lenora nodded.

"Good! My friends call me Kay," the *Sun* reporter continued.

"What did you want to talk to me about—Kay?" Lenora asked.

"I want to know what your friend, Beverly Gray, is doing," Kay said.

"We don't talk about that," Lenora replied promptly.

"What do you mean?"

"Just that. Beverly is a subject we don't discuss."

"She still lives with you, doesn't she?" Kay asked in surprise.

"She sleeps at the apartment and once in a while she eats with us," Lenora nodded.

Kay regarded the girl across the table with a frown. "What is going on? I thought you and Beverly were the best of friends?"

"There has come a coolness," Lenora said smoothly, not meeting the other girl's eyes. "Beverly has other interests."

Kay knew at once that Lenora was being deliberately flippant because she was hurt.

"Tell me about it," Kay urged. "I have a special reason for asking."

"Are you looking for a human interest story for the *Sun?*" Lenora demanded with a wry smile. The next moment she was contrite. "I'm sorry. That wasn't nice of me, but—there is nothing to tell. The Alpha Deltas suddenly have been dropped from Beverly's life. She is rarely home. She doesn't have fun with us any more. In fact, she rarely even talks to us. When we ask her what she has been doing she shuts up like a clam."

"You are sure you don't know where she is working?" Kay persisted.

Lenora frowned. "Why don't you ask her yourself?"

"Tell me about your job," Kay said, deliberately changing the subject. "You are a photographer on the *Tribune,* aren't you?"

While she listened to Lenora, Kay's thoughts were still busy with the memory of Beverly at Beechwood and she wondered what she could do to discover what was going on.

## CHAPTER VI

## *Followed*

THE night Larry left for England Beverly drove him to the airport and in the shadow of the great silver plane they said good-by.

"I wish you weren't going," she said. "I'll miss you." She couldn't say, as she wanted to: "Larry, I'm scared. I need you to help me. I don't know what I've stumbled into."

"I'll make it as brief as possible," he declared. "I'll hurry home—to you."

Then he was gone and she was alone—really alone. She shivered as she sat in the close darkness of her car and watched the wing lights on the plane merge with the stars in the sky. She was definitely on her own now. Gone was the comforting feeling that if she should get into trouble she could appeal to Larry for help. She had to accept and alone deal with anything that happened. It was not a comforting thought.

After a long while she went wearily home and found only Shirley there. The play was over and Roger had brought her straight home because she was tired. She was in the kitchen drinking a glass of milk when Beverly dropped into a chair at the table and rested her head in her hands. Her shoulders drooped with weariness and discouragement.

"Tired?" Shirley asked after a moment.

Beverly nodded.

"You aren't getting enough rest or eating enough," Shirley said. "But maybe I shouldn't say anything."

Beverly silently regarded Shirley's frowning face and she realized that she had put the frown there.

"Shirley—" she began impulsively. "Shirley, I—" There was a plea for understanding in her eyes, and Shirley did not fail her.

Shirley came around the table and put her arm about Beverly's shoulders.

"It's about time," she said. "I was beginning to wonder if it were really you or a mummy we were living with."

"I must go on being a mummy," Beverly said, holding her friend off, "but I don't like it."

"Never mind," Shirley said, accepting Beverly's refusal to explain her conduct. "I'll be the three little monkeys rolled into one—see nothing, hear nothing, and say nothing. Whatever it is, remember, Bev, there's a redheaded girl with a temper who is willing to stand up with you against anything."

"Stop it," Beverly said, touched, "or I'll cry. I don't deserve you, Shirley."

"Of course not," Shirley agreed smoothly. "I ought to get the rolling pin after you for letting us think you had suddenly gone high-hat over your successful play—"

"Is that what you thought?" Beverly asked aghast. "I never dreamed anything like that—"

Shirley nodded. "I know, but there were times—"

"Perhaps some day I can explain," Beverly said.

"We'll take you on faith," Shirley smiled. "You might know the Alpha Deltas would never forsake you."

Abruptly Beverly fled from Shirley's presence, nearly

knocking Lenora down as she swept through the kitchen doorway.

"Well!" Lenora exclaimed. "Cyclones are early this year."

"Shut up!" Shirley said, blowing her nose and brushing away a tear.

"What did she say to you to turn on the waterworks?" Lenora inquired suspiciously. Her eyes lighted. "Did she explain what has been the matter these past weeks?"

Shirley shook her head. "No. Have some milk?"

"I don't want any milk," Lenora said firmly. "I want a fortuneteller with a crystal ball so I can discover what is wrong with Bev."

"Let her alone and mind your own business," Shirley advised.

"That is a new tone for you," Lenora said in surprise. "A few days ago you were all for investigating her behavior."

"I've changed my mind," Shirley replied.

Lenora thoughtfully considered her friend. "I've known you a long while, Shirley. I believe we understand each other. What did Beverly tell you?"

"She didn't tell me anything," Shirley insisted. "I told

her that no matter what was wrong, her friends were behind her and if she were in trouble she could always count
on us."

"She knows that," Lenora said. "It doesn't seem lately,
though, as if she wanted her friends."

"That isn't so!" Shirley flew to Beverly's defense. "I
know you were hurt when she left the *Tribune* right after
you got a job on it and wanted to work with her, but I'm
sure Beverly will be back with you some day. She hasn't
said so, I just feel it."

"I hope you are right," Lenora sighed, "but you'll for-
give me, won't you, if I say I don't believe it?"

The next day Beverly was in the garden at Beechwood.
Kresloff had told her she might cut some of his roses to
put in a vase on her desk if she so desired. Beverly secured
shears from Forrest and was about to cut a beautiful
golden yellow bud when she heard a faint buzzing noise.
At first she thought it was a bee, but she could not see any
on the flowers close to her. The sound persisted, growing
in volume and then diminishing, only to grow louder
again as Beverly moved toward the rear of the house.

Then she saw it, a tiny motor-driven model airplane.
It soared over the lilac bushes and dipped gracefully as it

was caught in the light breeze. The white of the wing-spread gave it the appearance of a sea gull. Except for the small whirring propeller it might have been a bird, she thought. Across the lawn stood Kresloff, glancing repeat-edly from the plane to his watch and back again.

The plane circled gracefully, swooping low over the flower bed, as if in homage to its beauty. Then it climbed high into the sunshine again, and quite suddenly disap-peared. One moment it was there, a tiny thing of wood and paper, and the next instant there was nothing but a white puff of smoke.

Beverly looked across at Kresloff again. He was turning away, a contented smile on his face.

Beverly stared, fascinated, at the spot where the little plane had disappeared. There had been no noise, nothing. One moment it was there, the next moment it was gone. Even the tiny cloud of smoke had disappeared. There was nothing but empty sunshine.

She shivered suddenly as if a cold hand had touched her. What did it mean? What happened had taken place right before her eyes, and yet she could not explain it. Forgotten were the flowers she had planned to cut as she went into the house and up to her office. Here at last was something important, something to report to Lieutenant Petersen, but *what* was it?

"Miss Gray, will you please deliver these flowers for me to Mrs. Portage? You know her address." Kresloff stood in the doorway, a long green box in his hands. "There will be no need for you to come back here today. I'll see you tomorrow morning."

The Countess! All the way into town Beverly worried about being recognized, but her problem was solved when a maid came to the door of the Fifth Avenue mansion. Beverly gave her the flowers and climbed back into her car. She drove to the apartment and found a telephone message from Jim Stanton, asking her to meet him for dinner. For several weeks Jim had been home in Renville, and Beverly was eager to hear news of her friends there.

She left her car in the garage and walked across town to the restaurant Jim had suggested. He was waiting for her, and offered her a corsage of violets with a gallant flourish.

"I'm sorry I couldn't call for you at the apartment," he explained. "I had an appointment with my boss that left just enough time for us to meet here, eat, and get to the Ice Show in time for the opening."

"Quite an evening!" Beverly exclaimed.

"I have been commissioned by your fiancé to watch out for you while he is away, so I have a good excuse to plan something for every night in the week," he answered brightly.

"Tell me about Renville," she commanded. "What is the latest gossip?"

"Well, someone has broadcast the fact that one Beverly Gray has written a hit play and everybody is boasting about how he or she knew you when."

Beverly blushed becomingly and nodded to him. "My press agent!"

"Your parents are mighty proud," he declared. "And so are all the members of the Lucky Circle. Remember that old gang, Bev?"

"Of course!" she exclaimed. How well she recalled each member of the happy group she had known since before schooldays.

It was a very pleasant evening she spent with Jim, and the warm memory of it made the next day seem more bright. However, the morning of the following day her bright mood was abruptly shattered.

When Beverly arrived at Beechwood the gateman

handed her the morning newspaper to take with her to the house. She could not help but see the headline:

MAIL PLANE MYSTERIOUSLY DISAPPEARS

She parked her car in its accustomed place and remained behind the wheel to read the brief account.

"A search is being made for the U. S. mail plane en route to California. Nothing has been heard from it since it took off at Washington yesterday, nor has there been any report of a plane crash. It is as though the clouds had swallowed it completely."

Beverly looked up, across the lawn, remembering another plane that had disappeared. It hadn't been a mail plane. It hadn't been important at all, but it, too, had disappeared as if the clouds had swallowed it.

Quickly she seized the paper again and began scanning page after page. At last she gave a soft exclamation of satisfaction. It was just a small note on the society page to the effect that Mrs. Dwight Portage was enjoying a brief visit in Washington.

The Countess was in Washington! Before she went Kresloff had sent her flowers—on the same day of the model plane episode. Now a mail plane had disappeared after taking off from Washington. Were all these things tied together in some unseen fashion?

Slowly she got out of the car and started toward the house. The path led past the laboratory and as she came opposite the door, Kresloff came out, holding one hand aloft. Blood was gushing from a wound in his forearm and already his clothes were splattered with it.

"Mr. Kresloff!" Beverly cried.

"Call Doctor Long quickly," he gasped, starting to run toward the house.

"Wait!" Beverly cried. "Your arm—"

She went close to him and boldly and swiftly seized his necktie. In a moment she had it tied around his arm and a twig inserted to keep the tourniquet in place. The doctor came at once and after attending to his patient, commended Beverly on her first aid.

Kresloff then gave Beverly instructions to go into town and get some things for him, and ended with:

"I shall not forget what you did this morning, Miss Gray."

He did not mention what had happened in the laboratory to cause the wound, and Beverly did not ask any questions. On her way to her car, she paused at the laboratory and stepped inside. She shut the door and switched on the electric light. Since there was no way in which any telltale light could escape to reveal her presence, she could look around in safety.

She came to a table by the wall and viewed the shattered glass instruments thoughtfully. He probably had dropped something heavy into their midst and the flying glass had caught him on the arm. However, there was nothing to indicate what had caused the damage.

As Beverly guided her car into the right-hand lane of bridge traffic she noticed a black sedan pull in behind her. She recognized it as the same car which had been behind her all the way from Beechwood. Was it a coincidence, or was it following her?

Beverly had decided to go to Lieutenant Petersen and tell him the suspicions she had about Kresloff, the model plane, the Countess, and the mail plane. The Lieutenant had warned her not to come to him unless absolutely necessary, and then only if she were sure no one would know she had seen him. She had submitted a weekly written report to him addressed to a post office box, but now she wanted to talk to the man, to discuss her problems, and receive his advice. Just writing a report that went unacknowledged was highly unsatisfactory. But now, if **she** *were* being followed, it would be impossible for her to **go** to the Lieutenant.

When she left the bridge she turned off into a **small** side street, followed that for a block, and turned into **another**. She went through a maze of streets and always **the** black car followed her.

Beverly stopped first at the tiny chemist's shop to which Kresloff had telephoned an order. The package **was** wrapped and waiting for her and when she returned to her car, she saw the black car parked about a half block behind hers.

Her next stop was at a bookstore to secure some books for Kresloff and here, too, the black car waited where the driver could watch her.

What should she do? She could not go to Lieutenant Petersen with one of Kresloff's men on her trail. Why should Kresloff have her followed in the first place? Had she committed some error that made him suspicious? She had no idea what it might be. She had tried to be extremely careful.

The more she thought of it, the more anxious she became to communicate the threads of information she **had** to Lieutenant Petersen. Perhaps he could fit the pieces of the puzzle together. But how could she reach him? If she herself could not go to him, someone would have to go for her.

Shirley! Shirley could do it. Shirley had promised not to ask questions. She could be trusted to carry a message. From a telephone in the bookstore Beverly called her friend and asked her to lunch. Shirley accepted at once, although her voice sounded surprised.

Beverly met Shirley a half-hour later and they had lunch in a large restaurant on a prominent corner on Broadway. Beverly deliberately had chosen the popular spot in order to quell her follower's suspicions. It must appear like an innocent luncheon engagement.

"Beverly," Shirley leaned across the table when they were about to start on their dessert, "isn't there something you wanted me to do? You asked me to meet you for lunch and yet you have scarcely spoken all the time we've been here."

Beverly smiled and shook her head. "You are doing something by just having lunch with me."

She realized now, clearly enough, that she could not ask Shirley to take any message to Lieutenant Petersen. The

Lieutenant had insisted upon strict secrecy. Also Shirley might be placed in a dangerous position. It would not take Kresloff long to discover Shirley had been the messenger. Beverly rejected the idea in favor of her friend's safety.

The girls finished lunch and parted on the sidewalk. Beverly drove slowly back to Beechwood and, as on the way into town, the black car was as inescapable as her shadow. She had an almost irresistible urge to turn around and run as she drove into the grounds of Beechwood, but it was too late. The gate shut behind her and she had to go on to the house as if nothing were wrong. Her heart was heavy with foreboding. Kresloff must know she was a spy. For what other reason would he have had her followed? She had failed Lieutenant Petersen.

Beverly stepped into the cool hall and walked to the stairs, her heels tapping on the polished floor.

"Miss Gray!"

She had taken only two steps when the library door opened and Kurt Kresloff called her.

"Come in here, please."

Slowly, feeling as if the end of the world had come, Beverly went into the library and took the chair he indicated. He sat down across the desk from her and picked up a gold paperweight, fingering it absently, his eyes studying her until she felt warm color staining her cheeks.

"Miss Gray, where did you go today?"

"To town," Beverly answered mechanically.

"I know. I mean, where in town?"

"To the chemist's shop and to Sutton's bookstore. Your things are in my car."

"Did you do anything else?"

"I don't understand," she began, recovering herself a little. "What difference does it make—"

"Please, Miss Gray."

"I had lunch with a friend and drove back here."

When she had finished he picked up the telephone and spoke into it.

"Karl, you followed Miss Gray today. What did she do?"

While Beverly sat in silence, thanking her lucky stars she had told the truth about her actions, Kresloff listened to the voice on the telephone. At last the crackle of the voice stopped and he replaced the receiver. Then he got up and walked to the window and stared out into the garden.

"It seems I have done you an injustice, Miss Gray."

Beverly swallowed hard. "How do you mean?"

"I did not trust you," he said frankly. "Because my work is so important—so vital—I am suspicious of everyone. You may smile if I tell you my work will one day affect the whole world, but I assure you I am not boasting. Some day I shall be the most important man in the world."

Was he joking? Beverly wondered. His words were either a joke or the dream of a madman.

"What was I suspected of?" Beverly asked in a faint voice.

He shrugged and smiled. "Of being one of those against me."

"Why did you think that?" Beverly asked. "What did I do?" she thought frantically. "I tried to be so careful!"

"I told you, I am suspicious of everyone," he said. "I apologize and now you may go back to your work."

Beverly felt herself dismissed. He bent over the letters on his desk and somehow she could not trust herself to speak again. She got up from her chair, her knees trembling, and walked to the door. There was no sound from the man behind her, but she felt his eyes boring into her back. She went out of the library and upstairs into her own room. There she sank down on the window seat and breathed deeply of the warm afternoon air. What a narrow escape that had been! Had she really escaped? Was he less suspicious of her now? She wondered about that as she sat down at her typewriter and inserted a sheet of paper.

A stack of pencil notes was placed neatly beside the machine and she began automatically to copy them, page after page, until she reached the fourth. There, exactly the same size as the others, but in a different handwriting, was a page containing the words "Be careful!" She knew at once it was meant as a warning to her, but from whom? How did it get there? She tore the sheet into tiny shreds and stored them in her handbag to be disposed of the moment she left Beechwood. The words, "Be careful!" though they were both a warning of danger and an admonition, were heartening. It meant an unseen and unsuspected friend was near.

## CHAPTER VII

## *Plans*

LENORA, after much deliberation, went to the telephone and called Katharine Merrill at the *Sun* office.

"It's my turn now," she said. "How about meeting me for lunch?"

Kay accepted and they met at the appointed time and place. They were no sooner seated in the restaurant than Lenora began:

"Now I want to ask you about Beverly."

"Me?" Kay looked surprised. "Are you worried about her?"

Lenora nodded.

"It's about time," Kay said dryly. "I wondered how long it would take you to see beyond the end of your nose. You should be ashamed of yourself—letting anything come between you and Beverly."

"I know," Lenora murmured, coloring. "I guess it was because we were such good friends I became jealous of anything she did in which I wasn't included. I know I was unjust, but now I want to know what's going on. I have an idea you can help me."

"Beverly's the one who will need help," Kay said. "At least she will if what I suspect is true."

"What is she doing?" Lenora asked, her voice tense.

"She is playing with fire—or, more likely, dynamite," Kay said ruefully. "She is wading into trouble with both feet and won't let anyone go with her."

"Why? How?"

"Did you know she is Kurt Kresloff's secretary?" Kay countered.

"Kresloff!" Lenora exclaimed. " 'The Man Who Hates Cameras'?"

Kay nodded. "I see you remember him."

"Of course," Lenora nodded. "Beverly—his secretary! I don't understand."

"It doesn't make much sense, does it?" Kay agreed. "A good reporter like Beverly wasting her time typing notes and answering the telephone. I couldn't believe it either."

"But Beverly's not a secretary," Lenora protested.

"She is now," Kay replied. "I saw her there myself."

Lenora took a bite of lunch slowly and considered what Kay had said. "She is up to something, of course."

Kay nodded in agreement.

"But what?" Lenora asked next. "If you know anything, Kay, please tell me."

"She wouldn't tell me a thing when I asked her about it," Kay said unhappily.

"What do you suspect?" Lenora continued eagerly.

"Well," Kay took a deep breath and began. "Ever since that first explosion out at Kresloff's laboratory I've been interested in the man's history. No one seemed able to tell me anything about him. That only made me more curious. Everybody seemed to accept the fact that he was a famous scientist, but why was he famous? What had he done? Where had he come from?"

"I've wondered the same thing myself," Lenora commented. "Go on."

"I went to see the real estate firm from whom he bought his property. They couldn't tell me anything beyond the fact that he had paid cash for it. That made me curious, too. For a man to calmly hand over thousands of dollars in cash—where did he get it?"

"I began to ask questions about him in scientific circles and at last I met a man who had known him in Europe. He told me Kresloff had been interested in chemical research in several universities in Vienna and Paris, and when he had last seen him, Kresloff had his own laboratory in London."

Lenora listened intently.

"That left me nowhere," Kay shrugged. "Apparently he was just what he seemed. Still, I wasn't satisfied. I cabled to our press representative in London for all the information he could give me on Kresloff. I have his reply here." From her handbag Kay drew a much folded and worn cablegram. She handed it to Lenora and waited while the other girl read it.

"Kresloff mystery man. Scotland Yard says dangerous to government. Experiments with explosives."

"It doesn't say much," Lenora commented at last. She returned the wire to Kay and was silent for a few moments, forgetting to eat. "It will probably be a humdinger of a story," she sighed.

"Probably," Kay agreed with a nod.

"She shouldn't be there alone," Lenora offered next. "I wonder if she knows this?"

"I told her," Kay said, "but I don't know if she believed me. She may have thought I was just after a story."

"Maybe if we both went to see her there—" Lenora suggested. "I wonder how we could get to her. Kresloff wouldn't let reporters on the grounds."

"We could climb the wall," Kay murmured in joking fashion.

"Yes," Lenora nodded. "We could."

Kay considered it for a moment. "Why not?" she asked at last. "Let's go."

They went out into the gray, warm afternoon. A storm was hovering over Manhattan. Already the tall spires of buildings were wrapped in mist.

"It is going to pour any minute," Lenora declared with a glance at the sky.

"You won't melt," Kay laughed. "Come on, I think a bus leaves in five minutes."

The girls had no definite plan of action. All they

wanted was to find Beverly and somehow make her tell
them what she was up to. After that, perhaps, they could
plan.

"She might refuse to tell us anything," Kay said
thoughtfully.

"She might," Lenora agreed, "but on the other hand,
she might be glad to see us."

The summer evening was long, and though storm
clouds were low, there was still enough light for the girls
to see clearly. They walked back from the bus stop, past
the estate with its high stone wall. There were only two
gates in the wall and they were both locked. In addition,
the gate in front had a watchman stationed at it.

"How did you get in the first time?" Lenora asked.

Kay laughed. "I bluffed my way past the guard, but
I'm afraid it wouldn't work a second time."

"Well, I guess we'll have to climb it," Lenora declared,
regarding the wall with a frown.

Kay nodded. "The most likely spot would be down at
the corner where the grass is high and there are trees on
both sides."

They walked along close to the wall, disturbing insects
and birds. An occasional rabbit hopped out of their path,

and squirrels peered at them from the tree under which they finally stopped.

Lenora tried unsuccessfully to find a foothold in the wall. Ivy and moss made the rocks slippery, and finally she had to give up.

"Perhaps we could climb the tree and work our way out on the branch far enough to step onto the top of the wall," Kay proposed.

"I'll try it," Lenora said. "Give me a boost."

It took her about ten minutes, but finally she beamed down at Kay from her perch atop the wide stone wall.

"Come on up, the weather's fine," she invited.

Kay was not quite as agile as Lenora, but she finally managed it and together they considered the garden within the wall. First Lenora, and then Kay, dropped to the smooth carpet of grass. They crouched close to the wall until they were sure no one had seen them.

"Now that we are here, what are we going to do?" Kay demanded.

"Find Beverly," Lenora answered simply.

She led the way past the long row of rhododendron bushes to a narrow flagstone path that skirted the laboratory and led to the house.

"Do you propose to walk in the front door?" Kay asked with an amused smile. "Kresloff might decide to have us arrested for trespassing."

"Where do you think you are going?"

Both girls wheeled at the sound of Beverly's voice coming from the bushes close to the laboratory.

"Beverly!" Lenora exclaimed. "Are you all right?"

"Of course I'm all right. What are you doing here?"

"We came to see if you were in trouble," Lenora replied. "Bev, Kresloff is a dangerous man. He works with explosives and he had to leave England—"

"How did you know I was here?" Beverly interrupted.

"I told her," Kay put in. "We thought you might need some help in getting a story out of Kresloff."

"You had better leave before he sees you," Beverly advised. "How did you get in?"

"Over the wall," Lenora grinned. "Aren't you glad to see us, Bev?"

Glad to see them when their presence so jeopardized the work she had to do?

"No," Beverly said firmly. "I wish you'd go—at once."

"We had grand ideas about rescuing you from the villain's clutches," Lenora began, "but if you like it here—"

Beverly made no reply, merely led the way back along the path to the wall where they had come in.

"I appreciate your thoughts," she smiled, "but if you are seen here, you will do more harm than I can tell you."

With Beverly's assistance, the girls got back atop the wall. Beverly waited until she heard them safely down on the other side and then she started back toward the house. When she first saw them enter the garden, as she stood at the window in her office, she scarcely could believe her eyes. She had raced down to intercept them before Forrest or Kresloff should see them. Now, as she walked back, she felt almost weak with the narrow escape they had had.

She entered her office and started with surprise as Kresloff rose from the window seat where he had been waiting for her. The shadows were lengthening and from the dark sky outside came a short rumble of thunder. Beverly snapped on the light and the glow dispelled some of the uneasiness she had felt on seeing Kresloff.

"Miss Gray," he began at once, "I am leaving in a few moments on a short business trip. I want you to stay here in my absence. I expect a very important package and I do not want it to fall into the wrong hands. I want you to receive it and keep it safe for me. I have had the guest room next to this made ready for you. You can send Forrest for anything you might need. I should be back sometime day after tomorrow."

In another moment he was gone, giving her no opportunity to comment on his orders.

A flash of lightning outside revealed that the rain had started. Beverly crossed the room to close the window and she was just in time to see Kresloff step into his car and drive off.

# CHAPTER VIII

## The Thief

---

THE house was silent with the deep, enfolding stillness of midnight. Beverly lay in the small comfortable bed in the green and white guest room and stared at the ceiling. She had gone to bed shortly after her solitary dinner, served on a tray at her desk. It had rained for hours. The sound of the rain beating against the windows had been, somehow, comforting, but now even that had stopped. There was no sound anywhere in the house. It was as if the very shadows were waiting for something. The silence was becoming oppressive. All she could hear was the beating of her own heart.

Right after Kresloff had left Beechwood, Beverly had telephoned to the Alpha Deltas' apartment. Lois had answered the telephone and agreed to pack a small overnight bag for Beverly, which she had given to Forrest when he had called at the apartment for it.

The hours of the night went slowly. Beverly slept at last, but she was awake when the first rays of the early sun timidly shone in her window.

Though the household staff consisted of Forrest and two maids, Forrest always had waited upon Beverly. However, this morning a small, thin, freckle-faced maid brought her breakfast tray.

"Where's Forrest?" Beverly asked as the maid poured her chocolate.

"He went out last night, Miss, and hasn't come home yet," was the reply.

"Oh," Beverly said. "Is that unusual?"

"Oh, yes! If Mr. Kresloff knew Forrest had been gone such a long time—I mean, leaving the house unprotected, as you might say—Forrest would lose his place," the maid declared.

"Mr. Kresloff would discharge him?" Beverly asked.

"Oh, yes, Miss. You won't tell him, will you?" The

maid regarded Beverly in alarm, realizing she might have talked too much.

"No," Beverly said. "I won't tell him."

After breakfast Beverly walked from the house to the high iron gate to get the morning paper from the gate-man, then she returned to the house. A small item on the front page stated that an investigation into the disappear-ance of the mail plane was going ahead rapidly. Once more all her suspicions returned to puzzle her. If only she could learn something definite which would either prove or disprove her theories!

The morning was long, spent in idleness, and after lunch she went to her office determined to do something to shorten her stay at Beechwood. She just could not stand many more days of living in constant suspense. It was like walking around the rim of a volcano, afraid of falling in.

Beverly thought again of the frequent short notes she typed to members of Kurt Kresloff's Charity Committee. Could there have been anything in them? Anything which was masked by the obvious innocence of their ap-pearance? She went to the filing cabinet and got out a copy of the notes she had written during the past several days. The top one looked innocent enough. Apparently it was just a summons to a meeting to prepare for the bazaar which they hoped would yield a large return for the Children's Hospital.

Beverly left the letters on her desk and walked to the window to stare out over the garden. It was quiet and peaceful in the afternoon sunshine, yet every time she looked at it she visioned a tiny airplane that disappeared in a wisp of smoke before her very eyes.

Lieutenant Petersen and those behind him were certain there was some ulterior purpose in Kresloff's presence in this country, in his experimental work, yes, even in the seclusion in which he worked. She had been assigned the task of discovering what that purpose was, and so far she had failed. Kresloff was courteous, hard-working, and generous. He did not demand too much of her.

Beverly sat down again at her desk and considered the note on top of the pile of correspondence. It was short and to the point. Kresloff did not waste words. Could there be a code message contained in the few sentences? She tried rearranging the words, but without success. Then she tried every third word. That, too, yielded nothing. When she tried every second word she stared, fascinated, at the result.

"Meeting tonight to plan action. Need plans of all stations."

By pure chance she had stumbled upon an important discovery. She was no expert at such things. During schooldays, she and Lenora used to attempt such puzzles for amusement. Now, in idly studying the note, she had come upon a real, hidden message. Heartily she turned to the next note, copying down every second word. However, this time the words she chose had no meaning. It was evident that in this note the code was different. She went back and studied the first note. What had been the key that she inadvertently stumbled upon? Every other word. Every second word. Second! Two! The date was the second of the month! The second note was dated the fourth, so she tried every fourth word.

"Time is near. We must not fail. Remember our goal. Have patience."

How sure Kresloff had been of himself to adopt such a simple code! How certain he must be that he would not be discovered, that there was no danger of anyone else understanding his messages.

Beverly went through the file, seeking out each secret message. Only one or two notes did not yield one. Perhaps the code in them was more complicated. She would not waste time on them, but would turn them over to Lieutenant Petersen. She took the file of notes and a list of the names and addresses to whom she had delivered them, and left the office.

On the stairs she met Forrest. The encounter brought back at once what the maid had told her about his being out all night. He bowed to her and stood aside to let her pass, his eyes on the portfolio under her arm. She nodded in return and hurried to the door. Her one thought was to get to Lieutenant Petersen with her information before Kresloff returned. As she opened the door, the gateman and another man came up the path.

"This man has a package for Mr. Kresloff, Miss Gray," the gateman said.

"I'll take it," Beverly nodded.

After signing a receipt for the small, paper-wrapped parcel, Beverly went to her car. Kresloff had asked her to keep the package safe for him. She would—she would take it with her.

Beverly stopped at the entrance to the estate and waited for the man to open the gate, but instead he approached the car.

"I'm sorry, Miss, but I can't open the gate for you," the gateman murmured. "Mr. Kresloff left orders that no one was to leave the grounds for any reason whatever."

There was nothing she could say or do in the face of his orders. She went back to the house and sat in her office while she thought it over. The solution was, of course, the telephone. Did she dare to call Lieutenant Petersen? Was her information vital enough to ask him to come? She thought so. With Kresloff away was there still the danger of someone listening in on her conversation? She decided to take a chance and use the code the Lieutenant had given her. She had memorized the telephone number in Charlie Blaine's office that day. She dialed the number and waited, her heart beating rapidly. At last a man's voice said "Hello" very cautiously.

"Hello," Beverly echoed. "Is Mary there?"

"Mary?" The man repeated. "No, she isn't. Do you want to leave a message for her?"

This was all according to plan and Beverly felt relieved. Just the mere contact of a human voice, a friendly voice, heartened her.

"Yes," she said. "Will you tell her I have a present for

her? I can't deliver it, though, so she will have to come and get it."

"Very well, I'll tell her."

Beverly replaced the telephone and turned to see Forrest standing in the doorway. How much had he heard? Could he guess the meaning behind her words?

"What do you want, Forrest?" she asked, striving to keep her voice calm and natural.

"I came to see if you would like your dinner now, Miss," was the quiet reply.

"Yes," Beverly said. "In here, please."

When the butler had gone she paced up and down the room. How would Lieutenant Petersen answer her appeal? How soon could she expect someone to contact her?

Her dinner was delicious but excitement had stolen her appetite. She tried to read for a while but it was difficult to focus her attention on the printed pages. As it grew late and nothing happened, Beverly decided to go to bed. Probably she would have to wait until tomorrow before Lieutenant Petersen could reach her.

She undressed slowly and got into bed. The moonlight made a silvery path from the window to the door. She thought of Larry far away in England, and of the girls in the apartment. What were they thinking about her absence?

She must have dozed, because sometime later she awoke with a start and lay wondering what it was that had disturbed her. Something moved in the shadows by the closet. She was instantly wide awake. In tense silence she waited. The darkness there in the far corner was like a heavy black curtain.

With dismay Beverly remembered she had left her decoded copies of letters and the package for Kresloff lying on top of the dressing table. She had believed them safe enough there, but now there was a burglar—

Someone moved against the wall, stealthily, without noise, like a soft-footed animal. She realized that he was working his way toward the dressing table. He had not yet taken the package. In that case, she must stop him. If she screamed, would Forrest hear her and come to her aid? Or was it Forrest himself who was the intruder?

The pounding of her heart seemed to Beverly to be clearly audible anywhere in the house as she waited breathlessly for that mysterious shadow to move again. Her wrist watch loudly ticked away the seconds. It seemed years since she had first opened her eyes and made out the moving shadow. Now, again, the intruder moved slowly and carefully, evidently satisfied that Beverly still slept.

The instant the thief turned his back on the bed to face the dressing table, Beverly, the bedspread clasped tightly in both hands, leaped. The bedspread came down over the head of the intruder at the same moment Beverly let out a piercing scream. The thief struggled, desperation lending him strength, and finally, despite Beverly's actions, managed to throw off the cover. Beverly held on desperately, sure that help would come soon. The thief fought to get clear and with a final wrench tore himself free. Beverly felt her fingernails dig into soft flesh as the thief flung her from him and raced to the door. She reeled against the night table, sending the lamp to the floor with a crash. In another moment the thief was gone.

Beverly switched on the overhead lights and took one quick look at the dressing table. The package was still there.

"What is it, Miss?" Forrest was at the door.

"A thief," Beverly told him. "I caught him at the dressing table."

Even while she explained what had happened she wondered why, at this hour, Forrest should be as impeccably dressed as if he were serving dinner. Hadn't he been in bed? If not, why hadn't he come sooner in response to her scream?

## CHAPTER IX

### *Back Again*

---

WHEN Beverly stepped into the garden the next morning, the dew was still heavy on the grass and the sun had not yet reached the tops of the trees outside the wall. She walked slowly along the narrow path, breathing deeply of the cool morning air, letting it dispel the shadows and uneasiness which had hovered over her in the house. She felt she could not stand another night at Beechwood. She would not, either, if she had to sleep on the lawn!

Despite the early hour, Beverly saw the gateman coming toward her with a visitor in tow.

"A gentleman to see you, Miss."

"Mary sent me," the visitor offered.

"Will you come up to the house?" Beverly invited.

"I've come for Mary's present," the man said as he followed her into the hall.

Beverly's heart leaped. The man from Lieutenant Petersen! She looked at him more closely and could not help feeling disappointed. She did not know what she had expected, but inwardly she recoiled from this man. She did not like the dark, shifty eyes in his sallow face. His mouth had a surly twist, and his voice was harsh and unpleasant. Instinct told her not to trust him.

"Where's Mary today?" Beverly asked. If this man really had been sent by Lieutenant Petersen, he would reply by giving the address of the apartment where Beverly lived. If not—

"I don't know," the man said impatiently. "May I have the package now?"

"No," Beverly said, "I think not."

She had been right to be cautious. Her first impression of mistrust was true. He was not the secret service man. Someone must have listened in on her telephone call yesterday. That meant she could not use the telephone again.

The man realized at once that he had said the wrong

thing. He stepped close to her, his face angry, one hand seizing her wrist.

"Give me that package and no funny business!"

Beverly sought to pull away, but his grasp tightened.

"Is anything wrong, Miss?" Forrest loomed in the door-way of the library, big and solid-looking. Beverly had never been so glad to see anyone.

"Will you take this man to the gate, Forrest?"

For an instant she thought the stranger would resist forcibly, but Forrest was the larger of the two and he came forward with cool confidence. The stranger whirled and strode to the door. Forrest followed him out of sight.

Beverly sat down weakly on the stair steps. Things were happening far too quickly. Now what should she do? How could she get the information she possessed to Lieutenant Petersen so that he might take action?

From the messages she had decoded she had learned enough to know that Kresloff was working feverishly on some plan to make himself as he said, "the most impor-tant man in the world." What he planned when he reached that goal she could not guess. How he planned to achieve it was more vital to know right now. From his experiments and information she had gathered here, she surmised he planned to do it by destruction. If he had succeeded, as she suspected he had, in concocting a force so great it could make airplanes vanish, as the small model had, he could use it as a weapon to secure anything he wanted in the world. The world would be helpless before him. Beverly shuddered at the thought.

If Lieutenant Petersen knew of it at once, perhaps he could do something, but how could she get word to him? She could not telephone. She could not leave the estate—or could she? Lenora and Kay had come in over the wall. What was to stop her going out that way? She would go now—before Forrest returned from seeing the stranger off the estate.

Eager to take action, Beverly hurried upstairs, seized the precious package and file of letters, and hurried out of the house. She followed the little flagstone path that run behind the laboratory to the far wall where she stopped still in amazement. Sitting on the wall, like a modern Humpty Dumpty, was Lenora. She waved saucily to Beverly and swung her feet as she waited for the other girl to reach the spot below her.

"What are you doing here?" Beverly demanded. "Go home."

"Nothing doing," Lenora said flatly. "If a mouse can look at a king, as the fairy tales tell us, I can look at Kresloff. I have my camera," she added, "and I am going to come back every day until I get his picture."

"Why do you want a picture?" Beverly wanted to know.

"When the story you are on breaks, Charlie Blaine will want a picture of Kresloff for the front page. I aim to have it all ready for him," Lenora replied calmly.

"What if Kresloff sees you there?"

"Good!" Lenora said. "If he sees me, he will come close to ask me what I want. That's when I'll snap my picture. This time he won't get the camera plate either, because he'll be on one side of the wall and I'll be on the other." She waved a hand at Beverly. "Go about your business, chum, I don't mind sitting here alone."

Beverly shook her head in exasperation. It was just the sort of crazy thing Lenora would do.

"As long as you are here, help me over the wall."

"Why don't you go out the gate, it is simpler," Lenora suggested.

"I like to do things the hard way," Beverly retorted "Give me your hand."

With Lenora's help Beverly managed to reach the top of the wall. She sat down beside her friend for a moment.

"Are you going some place?" Lenora inquired.

Beverly nodded. "To town."

"Your car is still inside," Lenora reminded.

Beverly nodded again. "I'll take the bus."

"Are you coming back?"

"I don't know," Beverly replied slowly. "I don't know."

"Do you want me to go with you?" Lenora asked and held up a warning hand. "If you say 'No, thank you' I'll throw my camera at you."

Beverly laughed. "I must go alone."

"Okay," Lenora said cheerfully. "I might still be here when you get back."

The last glimpse Beverly had of the blond girl, Lenora was carefully dusting her camera. If Kresloff returned today, as he had said, Lenora might get her picture.

Beverly hurried along the narrow walk past the estate to the bus stop. All the way she had to curb the impulse to stop and look back. She wondered how long it would be before Forrest discovered her absence.

The bus came along almost at once, and Beverly climbed eagerly aboard. She was in the city in scarcely no time at all, or so it seemed, and she walked up Fifth Avenue, rejoicing in the familiar scenes: the crowds, the friendly smiles of policemen, the tall church spires against the blue sky. She had missed all this. It seemed as if she had been shut up within the walls of Beechwood for years.

At last she came to a gray stone building across from the park. An elevator took her to the tenth floor where a man in uniform asked her identity. In a few minutes she was standing at Lieutenant Petersen's desk and enjoying the delicious feeling of safety the warm room gave her.

"I brought Mary's present," she smiled, holding out the package and notes.

"I had arranged for one of our men to bring it in," the Lieutenant said in surprise. "Didn't he call for it?"

Beverly shook her head. "The only man I met was an impostor." Quickly she told him about the man who had tried to obtain the package that morning, about the thief in the night, about the little airplane, and about the Countess. The words tumbled from her lips eagerly, and with each one she felt the load on her shoulders lighten. She was passing the burden to broader shoulders, to wiser heads, and it was a great relief.

"Will you please wait, Miss Gray, while I see what this is all about?" Lieutenant Petersen picked up the brown parcel and disappeared through a door in the wall behind his desk.

Beverly wandered to the window and looked down at the green expanse of park. It was different than looking out her window at Beechwood. Here there was no stone wall, no undercurrent of mystery.

She smiled wryly as she thought of her determination of that morning not to spend another night at Beechwood. It seemed almost as if she were two people; one wanted to escape, to go as far away as possible from the unpleasantness of Kresloff and his experiments, while another spirit clung tenaciously to the task of fulfilling the mission upon which she had started. Was she the type that liked things only when there was smooth sailing? Would she walk out now that the going was becoming harder? She told herself firmly that she would see this thing through. She would do whatever Lieutenant Petersen asked her to do.

Beverly waited about thirty minutes. At the end of that time the Lieutenant entered again and handed her the same brown package.

"I want you to go back to Beechwood and give this to Kresloff when he returns—just as if nothing had happened," he said.

"Wasn't it important?" Beverly asked disappointedly.

He smiled. "Everything is important. Believe me, we appreciate what you are doing. You have supplied a lot of missing links in our knowledge. We know how hard it is for you, but it may not be much longer. I believe the end of the trail is in sight."

There were so many questions she wanted to ask. She was weary of working in the dark, but Lieutenant Petersen's quiet air of authority did not encourage questions. He walked to the door with her and smiled encouragingly.

"You are doing an excellent job, Miss Gray. Do you think you can carry on a little longer?"

To her surprise Beverly heard her own voice saying: "Of course I can!" And only that morning she had wanted to throw up her hands in despair!

"The most dangerous part is probably still ahead of you," the Lieutenant warned. "You must be careful. When Kresloff learns we are closing in on him, he will fight desperately. We will give you all the help and protection we can, but—"

"I understand," Beverly nodded. "It is still *my* job."

She went out into the sunshine and almost immediately bumped into Jim Stanton.

"Hi!" he exclaimed. "Where have you been? I've practically worn out the girls' telephone calling you."

"Sorry," she smiled, asking quickly, before he could question her further, "don't you ever work?"

"I'm on my way now," he replied. "How about lunch together?"

Beverly glanced at her watch and shook her head.

"Nope. I've got things to do."

"Dinner tonight, then?"

Again Beverly shook her head. "I might have to go out of town for a few days. Suppose I call you when I get back?"

With a wave of her hand she ran for a bus going downtown, leaving Jim staring after her in puzzled bewilderment.

The bus did not seem to go as swiftly on the way back to Beechwood as it had on the way to town, unless it was just her impatience that made it seem slower. Now that it was clear she had to return to Beechwood, she was anxious to get there before Kresloff did, and before Forrest became too suspicious of her absence.

Lenora was still perched atop the wall, a book open on her knees and a sandwich in her hand, when Beverly approached.

"You certainly come well equipped," Beverly laughed.

"All the comforts of home," Lenora nodded.

"Did you get your picture?" Beverly inquired after she had managed to climb up to her friend.

"There hasn't been a sign of anybody," Lenora sighed in disappointment.

"That's good," Beverly said, and carefully let herself down the other side of the wall.

"If you plan to do this very often you ought to provide a stepladder," Lenora declared.

The garden nodded sleepily in the warm sunshine, and the house looked cool and inviting as Beverly went toward it. Everything was quiet and serene. Beverly entered the hall and was going upstairs to her office when Forrest spoke from the threshold of the library.

"I have a message for you from Mr. Kresloff."

"Yes?" Beverly asked. "What is it?"

"He telephoned a little while ago," Forrest continued. "He asked me to tell you to bring the package which came yesterday to him at this address."

Forrest handed her a small slip of paper and Beverly stared at it in amazement. The address to which she was to take the mysterious package was Vernon College!

## CHAPTER X

### *Revealed*

---

It was a beautiful afternoon, there was not a cloud in the sky. Flowers clustered along the country roads and birds sang in the tops of gently swaying trees. The highway was an empty ribbon of white across the landscape and Beverly relaxed gratefully behind the wheel while her thoughts dwelt on her destination.

Vernon College. The Alpha Delta girls' alma mater. She thought of the shaded campus, the dignified coolness of the buildings, the ideals upon which the college had been founded. What possible connection could Kresloff have with Vernon?

When she arrived in the little college town it was almost like stepping into the past—back into the four happy years she had spent here as a student. It was always pleasant to return to this spot. Time never seemed to change it.

The campus was like a green velvet carpet laid at the foot of the gray, ivy-covered buildings. Flowers bordered the walks and birds kept house in the many trees.

Beverly parked her car before the new administration building and went into the office of the Dean. Though it was summer, and most of the students were gone, the school provided a summer program that kept many of the teachers and the Dean at work.

Miss Wilder had not changed, Beverly thought, as she sat across the desk from the Dean. She was a little thinner, perhaps, but she still had the same warm smile and the same friendly attitude.

"I'm looking for Mr. Kresloff," Beverly told the Dean. "He asked me to bring something to him here, but he didn't say where to find him."

"He is visiting Professor Larson and you will most likely find them both in the chemistry laboratory," the Dean said. "Mr. Kresloff came two days ago and the two of them have been bent over test tubes ever since."

"Professor Larson," Beverly murmured. "I don't remember him."

"He is new this term," the Dean explained. "He came to us when Professor Kline took a post in California. Professor Larson was highly recommended for his work in European Universities. Why he chose to work here at Vernon when he might have taken a more famous school I never understood."

Beverly remembered quite well that, though Vernon was a small college, it had one of the best equipped chemistry laboratories in the country. It had been lavishly bestowed by a former student who became rich and sentimentally wanted to do something gigantic for her alma mater. Was it possible Vernon had something even the great Kresloff did not have among his own test tubes?

"Stop in and see me again before you return to New York," the Dean invited when Beverly got up to leave.

"I will," Beverly promised.

She walked across the campus, deep in thought, until she was roused by a tennis ball hitting her on the shoulder.

"My goodness you walk fast!" A girl of Beverly's age hurried up. She was in white tennis shorts, racquet in hand, and she hugged Beverly exuberantly. "I tried to overtake you but you were too far ahead. You must even have gone deaf," Ada Collins accused, "because I called to you."

"I was thinking," Beverly apologized. "How are you?"

"Working hard," Ada returned promptly. "I love it here."

Beverly linked her arm within that of her friend. "Let's sit down somewhere for a few minutes. I would have words with thou."

They sat on the steps of Chadwick Hall, as they had done so many times when they were students, and exchanged news of all the Alpha Delta girls. Then Beverly asked the question she had in mind.

"What do you think of the new chemistry professor?"

"Professor Larson?" Ada murmured. "He is a queer duck. Has a beard and wears thick spectacles. He is a strict disciplinarian with the students, but he certainly knows his chemistry. Why do you ask? Don't tell me the teachers at Vernon get talked about in New York!"

Beverly laughed. "Miss Wilder mentioned him and I was curious. I have to see him and I wanted to know what to expect."

Ada rose. "You go about your business while I dress, then I'll meet you again before you go back to New York."

"At Wellers," Beverly nodded. "I still remember their enormous ice cream sodas."

Beverly went on to the chemistry laboratory. The building was quiet, the hall deserted. Her heels tapped smartly as she walked to the laboratory door at the end of the corridor. The door was locked but she fancied she saw shadows within, so she rapped and waited. After a moment a gray beard was thrust through a narrow opening. The beard was topped by hair of the same color, a small amount of brown face, and large, thick spectacles.

"Well?" Professor Larson demanded inhospitably.

"Is Mr. Kresloff here? He asked me—"

"Miss Gray!" Professor Larson was thrust aside immediately and Kresloff drew Beverly into the room. "Did you bring the package?"

Beverly handed the small parcel to him and he emitted a satisfied exclamation, turning to a table laden with test tubes to unwrap it. At last Beverly saw the mysterious contents of the package. She was disappointed. There was nothing spectacular about it. The bottle of liquid he extracted and held up to the light was colorless. Kresloff immediately uncorked the bottle and poured a few drops into a tube which was already full of a white powder. It smoked for a moment and then was quiet. It looked merely like a glass of milk.

"You shall see, Larson, that this will make me famous," he exulted, rubbing his hands together in gleeful satisfaction.

"Miss Gray will also see," Professor Larson said in a cold, hard voice that sent shivers up Beverly's back.

"Yes," Kresloff nodded. "I have told her something of it. She knows I have worked hard—"

"The readers of the *Tribune* will know it soon, too," Professor Larson continued harshly.

Beverly felt as if the world had suddenly rocked beneath her.

"What do you mean?" Kresloff snapped at his colleague.

"Miss Gray is a reporter for the New York *Tribune*," Professor Larson said. "I met her at a luncheon. She was one of the reporters sent to interview us scientists."

Kresloff whirled upon Beverly, his eyes blazing.

"Is this true? Is it?"

"I was a reporter before I took the position with you," Beverly managed to say calmly.

"And when you have learned about my invention you will go back to being a reporter!" Kresloff cried. His face was convulsed with rage and for a moment she thought he was going to hurl the contents of the bottle he held into her face.

"I suppose you confided all your plans to her," Larson taunted. "I suppose you told her how you hold fake charity drives and use the money for your own experiments? Did you give her the names of all of us who have helped you, risking our lives following your formulas? Maybe you even told her about the package you sent on that mail plane last week—"

"Stop!" Kresloff roared. "You talk too much, Larson. I always thought so." He paced up and down. "I must think what to do."

Larson reached over to pick up a test tube. As he did so, the sleeve of his coat pulled up and Beverly saw a long ugly scratch on his wrist. When she saw it she remembered vividly the burglar that had been in her room the night before. She could still feel her fingernails digging into flesh as the intruder pulled away from her.

"While we are clearing things up," Beverly told Kresloff, "you might ask Professor Larson why he tried to steal that bottle from my room at Beechwood last night."

There was a moment of utter silence, then Larson charged at Beverly like an angry bull. Kresloff intercepted him, white with fury.

"So that is where you went last night! You've been cheating me all along! You planned to take everything for yourself! Perhaps even your friend Mrs. Portage is cheating me!"

Larson laughed harshly. "She is working for me. She and I fixed that package so that it would explode in the plane. You wanted it to reach the research people in California, but we stopped you. If the police learn who sent it, you will be the one in trouble. You will never complete your experiments."

"I shall! I shall!" Kresloff screamed. "No one will stop me!" He picked up a stool and swung it at the chemistry professor who failed to dodge in time.

Kresloff stood over the fallen man muttering to himself. Suddenly he whirled and picked up the test tube into which he had poured some of the liquid from the bottle

Beverly had brought him. He added a little more liquid and set the tube upright on a table.

"Now we shall see!" he murmured. "In one hour this place will disappear. Like that!" he snapped his fingers. "And you with it, Larson!"

Beverly mentally shook herself to action and began to edge toward the door. So much had happened in such a short space of time, she had been stunned. Now it was high time to get away and call the police. Kresloff, in this state, was a madman.

She had barely reached the door when Kresloff saw her. With a strangled cry he seized her wrist and dragged her back into the room.

"You shall stay here, too. A reporter! Learning all my secrets! Now you shall learn my biggest. In there with you!"

He thrust her into the long narrow closet which held the chemistry class's supplies. He turned the key in the lock and though Beverly pounded on the door it was to no avail. Kresloff meant her to stay there, helpless, while the seconds flew past and the time for the explosion drew nearer. Once again, in her mind's eye, she saw the little airplane disappear in a puff of smoke. Would the same thing happen here? She sat down on a box of books to stop her knees from shaking. This was the chemistry laboratory at Vernon College. It would take more than a little test tube of chemical to make it disappear in a puff of smoke. Nothing like that could happen—not here! Not to her!

Once more she pounded on the door and only stopped when her hands were hurt and bruised. She tried shouting, but in the closed space her voice echoed loudly and weirdly in her own ears and finally she stopped. There were no windows and only one door—the locked one. It looked hopeless. There was an electric light and she switched it on, but it only served to keep her looking at her watch to see the swift passage of minutes, so she turned it off again and sat in still darkness.

One hour! Sixty minutes! Thirty-six hundred seconds! Her big adventure. Her last adventure. In a little while it would all be over.

"Beverly!" she said aloud, sternly. "Don't talk like that! And stop talking to yourself!"

"The most dangerous part is probably still ahead of you," Lieutenant Petersen had said. Could he have foreseen anything like this? She knew now the answers to all her questions. Kresloff had used the money he obtained through his "charitable" enterprises for his own ends. Larson and the Countess, alias Mrs. Portage, openly working for him, had secretly been aligned against him. Kresloff had sent a package of his precious chemical to California by air mail. Larson and the Countess had changed it, and the package had exploded while the plane was in midair, destroying the plane, and leaving Kresloff open to federal prosecution. She had the answers and yet she had to sit here, helpless, while Kresloff got away and went on with his plans.

Would someone, seeing her car still on the campus, come to look for her? Someone might, but not in time. Miss Wilder—Ada—they would give her longer than an hour to complete her business in the chemistry laboratory. One hour! It was such a short time.

Beverly could not resist a glance at her watch and reached up to snap the light on and off. Fifteen minutes of the precious hour gone! If only she could make time stand still! She had wanted that power before on several occasions, but they had been happy moments. They had been moments she had wanted to hold and treasure, enjoying happiness to the full, like the moment when she had received her diploma here at Vernon; the moment when she first knew Larry loved her; the moment when she knew her play had been a hit. She had wanted time to stand still then, but never so much as now. Never so desperately as now!

Larry! Larry! If only she had gone with him to England! If only she had told Lieutenant Petersen this morning that she wanted no further part in the adventure. If only! If only! Futile words. None of them helped now.

## CHAPTER XI

## *The Chase*

BOOKS, bottles, discarded test tubes. There was nothing to help her escape. The closet was becoming warm and stuffy. Once more she knocked on the door and then pressed her ear to the panel to listen for a sound from the outer room. Nothing but the beating of her own heart came to her.

Dejected, she leaned against the door. Must she accept the situation and do nothing? There was not much time left!

What was that? Her whole body tense, pressing tightly against the door, Beverly waited breathlessly for the sound to be repeated. Nothing but silence followed; however, she pounded again on the door and heard footsteps in the room outside. A moment later the door was flung open and Beverly fell out into the arms of Forrest, Kresloff's butler. For a moment she was too amazed to move, and he seemed to be just as astounded at seeing her. Then Beverly saw Professor Larson still lying on the floor and beyond him the fateful test tube!

"Professor Larson is responsible for the accident to the mail plane last week," she gasped to Forrest. "You had better turn him over to the police."

With that she snatched up the test tube and dashed for the door.

"Wait! Where are you going? Miss Gray—"

She heard Forrest's voice grow fainter behind her as she ran down the corridor and out of the building. Her one thought was to get away from the campus before the test tube exploded. There remained but seven precious minutes of the allotted hour. There was not enough time to wait and make explanations.

"Do or die for dear old Vernon!"

The words flashed through her mind as she ran. How often the girls used to chant them at basketball games and other sports. Now it might very well come true! Suppose the tube exploded while she held it in her hand? She gasped at the thought and hastened on.

Beverly continued past the last college building at the edge of the campus. Her objective was the uncared for plot of woodland beyond. There nothing would be harmed when the explosive did its deadly work.

· Beverly had just reached the edge of the woods when she heard a cry behind her. Kresloff! He had not fled. He had lingered to see the effect of his work. Now he had recognized her and what she carried. She saw him start after her and she plunged at once into the thickness of trees. Brambles scratched her; vines reached out to ensnare her; low-hanging branches slapped her as she rushed on, but she was conscious only of the man behind her. Less than five minutes now!

She heard Kresloff crashing through the brush behind her. She knew if he caught her there would be no escape for either of them. She planned, as she ran, to carefully place the explosive on the ground and escape, but her foot caught unexpectedly in a half-hidden root and she was thrown heavily to the ground. Stunned, she lay unable to move while precious moments fled.

Kresloff broke through the brush and dropped to his knees beside her, snatching up the tube from which most of the liquid had spilled. He looked at it and suspiciously sniffed the remaining drops. Then he flung it from him.

"Water! You emptied the bottle and substituted water! No wonder it didn't go off!"

No, she hadn't, but Beverly realized now that Lieutenant Petersen must have made the change. He hadn't let her go off with a dangerous chemical in her hands.

Suddenly she began to laugh uncontrollably. Her fears in the locked closet and her mad dash across the campus seemed so funny now. Nothing would have happened.

"Stop laughing!" Kresloff commanded.

"Miss Gray—" Forrest's voice came to them faintly.

"Forrest!" Kresloff exclaimed. "So he is in this, too!" He rose at once and slipped away among the trees.

"Miss Gray, are you all right?" Forrest came into sight and knelt anxiously beside her.

"Kresloff!" Beverly exclaimed. "He went that way. Catch him!"

Forrest darted away in pursuit of his employer and

Beverly followed more slowly. She had just reached the edge of the campus when she heard a car start. A second later a black sedan roared past with Kresloff at the wheel.

Forrest limped slowly from the woods on her right.

"I couldn't catch him. I turned my ankle."

Beverly looked at him sharply. Had he really injured his ankle, or was it a ruse to let Kresloff get away? Without another word, Beverly raced across the campus to her car. She would follow. If she could do nothing but keep him in sight, she would at least be able to let Lieutenant Petersen know where he went. They had not reached the end of the trail yet.

She drove off after Kresloff, over the back road from the campus, over a road full of ruts and hazy with a cloud of dust Kresloff's car had raised. At first she was glad for the dust. It made it easy for her to follow him, but then it began to get into her eyes and throat. She clung grimly to the steering wheel, sending the car ahead as swiftly as she dared. Once, as she rounded a curve, she thought she saw a black speck in the distance ahead of her and she increased her speed. However, Kresloff had had a good start and on the rough, uneven road it was impossible to catch up to him. By the time Beverly reached the smooth highway onto which the dirt road ended, he was lost in passing traffic.

She stopped her car and gave a weary sigh. What should she do now? Go back to Vernon and Forrest and Professor Larson? Or should she go on to New York and directly to Lieutenant Petersen?

She shook her head to her own thoughts. She had not reached the end of her adventure yet. This was not the end of the trail. That would not be reached until Kresloff was apprehended. She had been disappointed, but now she was coldly determined. She had taken this job and she would see it through at any cost. She would find Kresloff. Then, when it was all over, she would know she had done all she could. She would not have failed in any respect.

"Fine talk!" she jeered at herself. "Where will you find him, Miss Mastermind?"

Where would he go? As if in answer to her thoughts, she saw Kresloff's white, furious face as he looked at Professor Larson in the chemistry laboratory, and once again heard his words:

"I suppose Mrs. Portage is cheating me, too!"

There had been a vengeful light in his eyes when he said those words, and now, half-crazed with the frustration of his ambition, he would be capable of drastic revenge. He would want to hurt everyone who had hurt him.

Beverly started the car and turned onto the highway. She had no plan of action beyond the fact that she wanted to get to the Countess's apartment. What she would do when she reached there she did not know. Perhaps she would be in time to warn the Countess that Kresloff had discovered what had happened to the package on the mail plane. No matter if the woman was a spy or thief, she deserved to be warned against Kresloff.

Beverly was conscious of the dusty film of dirt on her car and her own soiled, disheveled appearance as she stopped before the swank apartment house and saw the cold eyes of the doorman regarding her disdainfully.

"Is Mrs. Portage in her apartment?" she asked as she got out of her car.

"I wouldn't know, Miss," was the haughty reply.

"And wouldn't tell me if you did," Beverly thought grimly, chafing at any delay. She went in the lobby and rang for the elevator. The same maid to whom Beverly had spoken once before opened the door to the Countess's apartment.

"No'm," she replied to Beverly's inquiry. "Mrs. Portage isn't home."

"Do you know where she went?"

"Yes'm. She went to that Mr. Kresloff's country place." With that the door was shut and Beverly stared at it unbelievingly for a moment.

" 'Step into my parlor,' said the spider to the fly," Beverly mumbled. The words brought her out of the daze and she whirled about to leave. The Countess was putting herself in the most dangerous spot she possibly could. She was walking right into Kresloff's hands!

The road to Beechwood had never seemed so long. Beverly drove with only half her mind on what she was doing; the other half was far ahead of her, in the library at Beechwood, imagining what was happening between Kresloff and the Countess. Afterward, she wondered how she ever completed the drive safely.

The gate to the estate stood ajar and the gateman was nowhere to be seen when Beverly drove into the grounds. She parked close to the gate, not caring to have Kresloff, or anyone else, hear the motor. She did not walk along

Beverly's eyes followed Lenora's gaze and she drew a quick, sharp breath of alarm. On the rug before the blackened fireplace lay a woman—the Countess.

Beverly's eyes followed Lenora's toward the black-curtained windows. The Southers

# CHAPTER XII

## *Escape*

---

In the silence of the library Lenora's whisper was ghostly.

"Bev, is she—is she dead?"

Beverly knelt beside the Countess and took the limp hand in hers. The pulse was steady, though weak.

"She has fainted," Beverly replied. "I wonder why."

Where was Kresloff? The question went round and round in her mind. What had happened here?

"Are you sure you didn't see Kresloff go out again?"

"Quite sure," Lenora murmured.

The house was silent all around them. The girls exchanged glances and once more looked about the room.

The very shadows in the corners seemed full of unnamed ghosts.

"Beverly, let's get out of here," Lenora whispered, an urgent hand on her friend's arm.

Beverly shook off the hand and approached Kresloff's desk. Some of the drawers stood open, papers in disarray. It was a rare opportunity. Heretofore, whenever she had stood at the desk it had been carefully locked—except, of course, when Kresloff had been sitting behind it.

"What are you doing?" Lenora asked in amazement as she watched Beverly seat herself in the big, swivel chair and methodically begin to search the drawers.

Letters with foreign postmarks, a bank book with an unbelievable balance entered in it, nameless formulas—all things which would be valuable to Lieutenant Petersen. Beverly gathered them together hastily. She must overlook nothing!

There was a sound from the fireplace and the Countess sat up dazedly. Both girls stared at her, then Beverly moved forward and helped her to her feet.

"What are you doing here?" the Countess murmured. "Where—where is Kurt?" She cast a fearful glance over her shoulder. Then her eyes came back to rest on Beverly.

She looked puzzled and Beverly knew the woman was remembering her.

"It has been a long time—Countess," Beverly murmured.

"Ah!" It was a long-drawn-out sigh. "You have an excellent memory, Miss Gray," the Countess said with a faint smile. "So *you* have been Kurt's secretary!"

Beverly nodded. "Where is he? What happened here?"

The Countess shook her head. "I have not forgotten that you are a newspaper woman. You would like me to give you the story, wouldn't you?"

"Yes," Beverly said, "but I will get it whether you give it to me or not."

"And the police—" the Countess murmured. "I suppose you have told them I am here?"

"I told them you were working with Kresloff," Beverly admitted.

"Beverly!" Lenora, realizing in a flash what Beverly had been doing the past weeks, let out a gasp which no one even heard.

Beverly and the Countess faced each other calmly. The older woman was shrewd, calculating. Beverly was clear-eyed and unafraid, determined to make this the end of the trail for the Countess.

"Suppose—suppose I tell you everything you want to know," the Countess proposed. "Will you let me walk out of here—free—before you call the police?"

"I can't bargain with you," Beverly frowned.

"Why not? Who will know?" The Countess moved closer to Beverly. "If I tell you what Kresloff has been doing—what he proposes to do—it will make an excellent story for your paper."

"I don't doubt it," Beverly agreed, "but I still can't bargain with you." She turned away. "Where did Kresloff go? I must find him."

"No!" the Countess cried, suddenly white and afraid. "No! Let him go. He is mad! Mad, I tell you. He is mad with ambition. He is creating a weapon that will make him the greatest man in the world!"

"He told me that," Beverly smiled, "but I don't believe it. What else do you know about it?"

Before the Countess could answer, Lenora let out a half-smothered exclamation.

"Beverly—look! The wall!"

A section of the book-lined wall was slowly swinging

inward. A moment later, as the three watched and waited, Kresloff stood in the opening.

"Where did he come from?" Lenora whispered.

"His laboratory," Beverly said. "There must be an underground tunnel leading to it."

"Right you are, Miss Gray!" Kresloff moved into the room. "I was preparing a little party for Mrs. Portage, but since you and your newspaper friend are here, you may join her." He walked to his desk and with one glance took in all the papers Beverly had gathered together. "It doesn't matter what you have seen," he shrugged. "You will never use it."

Lenora sat down abruptly in the nearest chair. The Countess huddled against the fireplace. Only Beverly faced the inventor squarely.

"You are very sure," she said with a faint smile. "Remember—your plans at Vernon went awry."

"And you were to blame for that," Kresloff exclaimed. "I have not forgotten. This time it will be different. I have personally taken care of everything."

"How?" Beverly wanted to know. She was talking for time. Why, she was not sure. An inner voice seemed to urge her to keep Kresloff talking.

"You shall have the honor of proving to the world just how effective my invention is."

"What did you invent?" Beverly asked bluntly.

He smiled. "The notes you typed for me, Miss Gray, were of experiments I have made. Now my work is almost finished. I have found a liquid more potent than nitroglycerin, greater than dynamite. Nations are bargaining for it. You have seen some of the letters here. I shall sell it to the highest bidder."

"In the wrong hands your invention could wreck the world," Beverly said, aghast. Lieutenant Petersen had been right. This man was a menace to the happiness and well-being of many people.

"Maybe it won't work," Lenora had forgotten her own fright in interest.

"On various occasions it has been proven," Kresloff told her. "Whenever one of my prospective purchasers demanded proof of its worth, such proof was given."

Beverly remembered the notes she had decoded. They had been about such things—plans for destruction of buildings, railroads, factories—

"But isn't it your patriotic duty to give such an invention to the United States Government?" Lenora inquired.

"I am not an American," he laughed. "I do not claim allegiance to any country." He selected three letters from among those on the desk and slipped them into his pocket. "The one who offers me the most shall receive my invention. And now I shall say good-by. I am sorry, Miss Gray, that you will be unable to write your story for the *Tribune*. I am sure it would have been very interesting."

"Kurt—" the Countess came forward. "You can't leave me here—to die!"

Kresloff looked at her coldly. "You and Larson were working against me. You wanted my invention for yourselves. You shall stay here with these newspaper people."

"My friend had nothing to do with this," Beverly said. "There is no reason for you to seek revenge on her. Chance brought her to Beechwood today—"

"With her camera?" he murmured. "Enough of this! Time is growing short. I shall—"

It was very faint—so faint as to be scarcely audible, but it was like a strong, sure light of hope to the girls in the library. A footstep! Overhead! Someone was walking on the second floor.

Kresloff, too, had heard and now he looked at his watch.

"Quickly! In here!" He herded the girls and the Countess hastily through the opening in the wall into the black narrow tunnel and swung the bookshelves shut upon them.

The Countess screamed and Lenora's hand sought Beverly's.

"Now what?" the blond girl asked in a whisper.

"I don't know," Beverly responded, straining her eyes to see through the blackness and her ears to hear the faintest sound.

"Oh, stop it!" Lenora exclaimed nervously as the Countess screamed again.

"Someone might hear," the Countess returned matter-of-factly.

Beverly smiled to herself. She had thought the Countess' nerves were gone when she screamed like that, but she was using the only weapon she had—her voice.

"Suppose we all scream?" Lenora suggested.

"It wouldn't help," Beverly sighed. "Kresloff has told me many times that the walls of his library are soundproof. Even if someone were in there with him, he would not hear us."

"How can we get out of here?" Lenora asked next.

"Through the laboratory," the Countess replied. "Come, let us hurry!"

She started off carefully, going slowly in the darkness, with Lenora and Beverly close behind her.

"If only we had a flashlight!" Lenora groaned.

"It can't be far," Beverly encouraged.

The Countess stopped so suddenly the girls behind her were thrown together.

"Go on! Go on!" Lenora urged.

"I can't," the Countess replied faintly. "This is as far as the tunnel goes."

Beverly and Lenora crowded past her to see for themselves. Their exploring hands touched nothing but dry, earthen wall.

"There must be more than one tunnel." Beverly endeavored to keep her voice calm.

"Are you sure a tunnel leads to the laboratory?" Lenora asked.

"I am sure," the Countess insisted. "Kurt has told me of it. This house is very old. During the Civil War the owner hid many things under the house."

"In that case there may be a tunnel leading to each room," Beverly said.

"How will we find the one to the laboratory?" Lenora wanted to know.

"Try them all," Beverly replied.

"Kurt said time was running short," the Countess reminded. "Something is going to happen and we shall not get out of here."

"Don't talk like that!" Lenora exclaimed. "We must get out!"

"Let's try another tunnel," Beverly proposed, starting back the way they had come.

"Don't get lost!" Lenora cautioned, hurrying to catch up with her friend.

Groping, hurrying, stumbling over loose pebbles and the uneven floor, time after time they came up against blank walls. Four times they had to admit defeat.

"It is hopeless!" the Countess insisted at last.

Even Beverly's stout heart began to doubt. Though she clung desperately to the hope that at last they would find the right tunnel, after four attempts—

"We can't even find the place we started from," Lenora added slowly.

"Let us rest for a moment," the Countess suggested breathlessly.

Beverly leaned wearily against the wall. She had been going at an unbelievable pace ever since morning—ever since last night, she corrected herself. Ever since she woke to find a burglar in her room. Was that only last night? She was ready to collapse from sheer exhaustion. Yet she did not dare give up. She still thought of the end of the trail. It had not yet been reached.

"Beverly—" Lenora spoke, close to her, groping through the darkness to touch her. "Beverly, what are you thinking?"

"How sorry I am that you are here," Beverly sighed. "You shouldn't have followed me, Lenora."

"I'm glad I'm with you," Lenora said stoutly. "Of course it would help if I knew what it is all about."

"Perhaps I can explain when we get out," Beverly said. "Come—let's try again."

The three started out close together, Beverly's hand on the wall, guiding them.

"Wait!" Lenora stopped. "Did you hear anything?"

"Mice!" the Countess muttered.

Lenora shivered. "I hope not!"

They moved forward until Lenora again called a halt. "I am sure I heard something! There it is again!"

There was the faint, indistinguishable sound of someone moving in the tunnel ahead of them.

"Hello, there!" A voice echoed hollowly down the tunnel. "Where are you?"

"Here!" Lenora replied loudly. "Who is it?"

Footsteps were heard running along the tunnel and a moment later the bright yellow beam of a flashlight swept over them.

"Are you all right?" a man's voice asked.

"Forrest!" Beverly exclaimed.

The light traveled from one to the other and then focussed on the floor as Forrest limped ahead of them.

"I don't know who you are," Lenora declared, "but if you can get us out of here I'll certainly believe in good fairies. How did you know there was anyone in the tunnel?"

"He is Kresloff's butler," Beverly told her friend.

There was a chuckle from the man leading them.

"That is who I have been for the past year. Allow me to introduce myself properly. I am Forrest Wells. My badge says number 42371."

"Secret Service!" Lenora exclaimed while Beverly took the revelation in more slowly.

"Of course!" she said aloud.

It would have to be! It was through him Lieutenant Petersen had learned Kresloff wanted a secretary, and all the times she had thought Forrest was spying on her—he had been, to be sure, but for her own protection. She might have known that Lieutenant Petersen would never have let her remain at Beechwood alone!

"Then you really did sprain your ankle at Vernon!" she exclaimed.

"Yes," Forrest replied, "unfortunately! But I got here in time to spoil Kresloff's little game. He had enough explosive in his laboratory to destroy everything for miles!"

"Where is Kresloff?" Beverly asked.

"Waiting with Lieutenant Petersen."

The bright light of the laboratory was almost blinding as the girls stumbled out of the tunnel into the room. Beverly noticed that some of the equipment had been broken, and she surmised that that had taken care of Kresloff's plan to destroy Beechwood.

"Lieutenant Petersen is at the house with Kresloff," Forrest explained, leading the way to the door.

Lenora followed directly after him, and then the Countess and Beverly. At the door the Countess turned.

"You will turn me over to the police," she stated, rather than asked.

"They have been looking for you for a long time," Beverly said.

"They will not catch me yet!" the Countess declared.

With one swift, strong movement she thrust Beverly back into the room, back against a table of half-filled bottles which tottered and crashed as Beverly fell against it. In a flash the Countess had shut the door from the outside while a light, grayish fog rose from the chemicals on the floor near where Beverly lay.

## CHAPTER XIII

## *The Countess*

THE bed felt deliciously comfortable and the smoothness of the pillow beneath her cheek was cool and soothing. Beverly sighed contentedly and it was then she thought she heard a satisfied murmur from someone else in the room. By opening one eye she could see Lenora and Shirley lounging on the other bed, while Lois stood near the window. All three were watching her.

"Good morning," Beverly murmured sleepily.

"Thank goodness!" Shirley sighed.

"I told you she would be all right," Lenora said loudly.

"Who?" Beverly inquired lazily.

"You," Lenora laughed. "How does the bump feel?"

"What bump?" Beverly raised herself up on her pillow and smiled at her friends. "Who has a bump?"

"You have," Lois supplied. "About the size of an egg."

Beverly put a hand to her head where, she became aware, little shooting pains were dancing back and forth behind one ear. She winced as her fingers came in contact with a good-sized lump.

"A little souvenir from the Countess," Lenora added. "Don't you remember?"

Beverly frowned. "Yes, I remember—part of it. What happened after the Countess locked me in the laboratory?"

"She got away in the darkness before any of us knew what was happening," Lenora explained ruefully. "You were ill—partly from hitting your head on that table and partly from inhaling fumes of the chemicals that were spilled. Forrest brought you home while Lieutenant Petersen took Kresloff to his office for questioning. He wants you there this afternoon—if you are able."

"Of course I am able," Beverly declared, sitting up.

"Are you sure?" Shirley interrupted. "All night long you kept talking about little airplanes that disappeared."

"I wish you'd explain what all this is about," Lois complained. "Shirley and I are in a fog!"

So Beverly told them as much as she thought she dared, after swearing them to secrecy about it.

"Lieutenant Petersen said something about picking you for the job because you knew the Countess and you knew Vernon College. They needed someone to tie everything together and you did it. You should get a medal," Lenora declared.

Beverly laughed softly. "It is enough to be back in favor with the Alpha Deltas."

Lenora shook her head. "I'm mad at myself for the way I acted. I should have realized there was something important afoot. It took Kay Merrill to bring me to my senses. When she wanted to know about you I began to add two and two together."

"I want to see Kay," Beverly smiled. "I can tell her about Kresloff now."

"She isn't so bad when you get to know her," Lenora commented. "I'll telephone her to meet us for dinner."

While Beverly dressed, Lois and Shirley prepared lunch, since it was far too late for breakfast, and Lenora went to telephone.

"The office hasn't seen Kay since yesterday morning," Lenora reported when she took her place at the table. "She isn't home, either."

"On a story, probably," Beverly said. "You've become pretty chummy with her, haven't you?"

Lenora nodded with a grin. "We called a truce between the *Sun* and the *Tribune* until you were once more back to normal. In fact, we were working together. We had a system. One day she would follow you and I would watch Beechwood. The next day we would change, and she would watch Beechwood while I trailed after you."

"A fine thing!" Beverly smiled. "Helping a rival reporter to spy on me!"

"We had just started the system," Lenora replied cheerfully. "She followed you yesterday. Didn't you notice her behind you when you drove to Vernon?"

Beverly shook her head. "No. I was too busy with my thoughts, I guess. If she followed me to Vernon, what happened to her? Why didn't I meet her there?"

"I can't imagine," Lenora said. "This salad is very good, Shirley."

"On behalf of my cook book, I thank you!" Shirley bowed.

"She is practicing for Roger," Lois giggled.

Beverly looked about at the smiling faces of her friends and she thought again how good it was to be here in the sunny apartment with friends such as these. The dark days at Beechwood were behind her. They would be swallowed up in the past as new days and new events took place, but she must still keep her appointment with Lieutenant Petersen to give him all the details she could about Kresloff's activities. Reluctantly she rose from the table.

"Let's do the dishes quickly so I can get to Lieutenant Petersen and back again. How about taking a nice long ride in the country tonight? You girls haven't tried out my car yet."

"We'll do the dishes—Lois and I," Shirley said. "You go along and keep your appointment."

"We'll treat you like company today and not make you dry dishes," Lois added smilingly.

"But—" Beverly began.

"Come on before they change their minds!" Lenora grabbed Beverly's hand and pulled her toward the door. "I'll walk to the garage with you and meet you at your car after you've talked to the Lieutenant. I have to buy a birthday present to mail to Terry."

As soon as Beverly was admitted to Lieutenant Petersen's office she knew something was wrong. Forrest stood by the window, a dark frown on his face. He nodded to her briefly and turned his attention again to Lieutenant Petersen who was talking on the telephone.

"Yes," Lieutenant Petersen said, in time for Beverly to hear, "keep searching. Report to me every fifteen minutes. We must find them!"

Beverly looked questioningly at Forrest.

"Larson," he said briefly. "He got away from the police yesterday at Vernon."

"There has been a report of a blue roadster in which a man and girl, answering their descriptions, were seen," Lieutenant Petersen said as he hung up.

"A girl?" Beverly asked. "The Countess?"

"We aren't sure," Forrest replied. "We think it was the reporter who met me as I started to follow you."

"Kay! It must be! Kay Merrill—she works for the *Sun*," Beverly explained as both men glanced at her curiously. "She was following me."

"That is who it must be," Lieutenant Petersen nodded.

"Larson probably is holding her as a hostage," Forrest added gloomily.

"Can't you do something?" Beverly asked urgently.

"We must find them first," Lieutenant Petersen replied. "We are doing our best." He pushed forward a chair. "Sit down. While we are waiting I will take your report."

They talked for two hours. During that time a report came every fifteen minutes on the progress of the search for Larson. None of them was encouraging. The man and girl in the roadster had turned out to be two entirely innocent people.

At last Beverly could sit still no longer. She left the office and went out to her car. Lenora was sitting there, reading a magazine while she waited.

"You look as though you are lost in a fog," she said cheerily as Beverly slid behind the steering wheel. "What gives?"

Briefly Beverly told her the latest news.

"We must do something, Bev," Lenora said at last. "It was really my turn to follow you yesterday, but I told Kay I didn't feel like chasing all over the map, and that I'd rather sit on the wall and wait. I feel responsible for her following you."

Beverly started the motor and turned into the line of traffic on the Avenue.

"Where are we going?" Lenora asked.

"To Vernon."

It wasn't quite clear what she expected they would do once they got there, but Beverly felt that, knowing Vernon as they both did, they might be able to help in some way. The miles slid away behind them and both girls were thoughtfully silent.

The college town was quiet and peaceful. No ripple of excitement stirred the sunny serenity which flooded the streets and houses. The afternoon sun glinted on the windows of the college buildings and swept the flower-bordered lawns with gold dust.

Beverly parked in front of the Administration Building and the girls went in to see the Dean; however, she had left that same morning for a week's trip. As they left the building, Ada Collins came striding across the campus toward them.

"A fine thing!" she teased Beverly. "You had a date with me yesterday, remember?"

"At Wellers!" Beverly exclaimed. "Ada, I'm sorry. So much happened—"

"I've heard about it," Ada laughed. "What brings you back today?"

"More of the same," Lenora told her. "Have you seen the villain that escaped? Or the girl he took with him?"

"A girl?" Ada asked. "One of the Alpha Deltas?"

"No. A reporter," Beverly explained. "The police are searching everywhere for them."

Ada nodded. "The law overran the campus last night and this morning, but eventually they went down into town and left us in peace."

"Perhaps we should talk to the police," Beverly suggested. "They might have learned something new since we left New York."

"We'll see you later," Lenora told Ada.

"I'll be in my room," Ada called, and waved as the car started to roll.

"Do you think there is much chance of Larson still being in Vernon?" Lenora asked.

"The police have not been able to find any clue which would show he left here," Beverly said. "They've taken his car. Only one train stopped last night and no one got on."

"If he is still here, why aren't the police hunting for him?" Lenora demanded.

"They are," Beverly assured her. "Lieutenant Petersen isn't overlooking anything."

"It doesn't look like a man-hunt to me," Lenora continued. "You see hardly anyone on the street."

"Let's have a milk shake," Beverly proposed, stopping the car in front of Wellers, a favorite spot of the college students.

"But, Beverly," Lenora persisted, dropping into a chair at a black-top table, "aren't you worried about what might have happened to Kay?"

"Certainly I am," Beverly replied. "I wonder, too, what has happened to the Countess."

"She is definitely a slippery character, isn't she?" Lenora declared.

"I hope I meet her just once more," Beverly murmured.

Lenora grinned. "You have a score to settle with her, haven't you? Does the bump hurt?"

"The only thing that hurts is my pride," Beverly said ruefully. "I don't know how I could so far have forgotten what she is to give her such an opportunity to get away."

The girls had their milk shake, remembering when they had often sat in this same room as students. As they emerged onto the street and climbed into the car, a woman passed them, walking swiftly, head down. She crossed the street directly in front of their car and it was then Beverly thought there was something familiar about the slender figure.

"Lenora!" she gasped. "It can't be! Look—tell me if I am dreaming. Is that the Countess?"

"It is! Beverly, it is!" Lenora said excitedly. "Where do you suppose she is going?"

"We must follow her," Beverly said, stopping the car immediately. "We can't drive because the car would be too conspicuous. She would be sure to see us."

"Hurry," Lenora urged, "or she will disappear."

The girls tumbled out eagerly and fell into step several yards behind the Countess. The woman walked swiftly, with head bent, not looking either to the right or left. She seemed to know where she was going and Beverly wondered how often before she had come to Vernon. To think that the sleepy little college town should be the setting for the final act in this drama! She had never thought her biggest adventure would end here in the shadow of the gray college buildings where so many other adventures had begun.

"Isn't this exciting?" Lenora murmured. "Us trailing

a fugitive from justice! It is just like something from a book."

Beverly laughed. "I don't understand how you got involved in all this."

"I involved myself," Lenora said with a chuckle. "I appointed myself your assistant."

Up ahead of them the Countess turned suddenly from the Main Street into a narrow lane that led out past the town into the countryside. There were few houses down this lane, and rarely any traffic.

"Do you suppose she is leading us on a wild chase?" Lenora wanted to know. "If we follow her down that road she is sure to see us. There is just open space on both sides of the road."

"You stay here and watch her as long as you can see her. I'll go back and get the car and take the road that joins this one at the fork a mile away. I'll come back and pick you up when I see which way she goes," Beverly told her friend, and began retracing her steps before Lenora could protest.

It was only a matter of minutes until she had driven down a side street and out on the country road which merged with the lane on which they had seen the Countess start. When Beverly paused at the junction, there was no one in sight. Slowly she drove down the narrow lane until she met Lenora waiting where she had left her.

"Did you pass the Countess?" Lenora asked excitedly.

"No."

"I watched until she went round the bend by the old mill down there," Lenora said, climbing into the car beside her friend.

"That means she is somewhere between the mill and the fork in the road," Beverly frowned.

Beverly drove back along the lane but, as before, there was no sign of the woman they sought. They stopped at the mill to talk over the situation.

"We passed two houses and this mill," Lenora murmured. "She must have gone into one of them. That is the only explanation."

"This mill has been deserted for years," Beverly said, "but shall we look here first?"

The creek which once had supplied water in enough force to turn the large wooden mill wheel had dwindled to a mere trickle now and the wheel stood idle, decaying with the passing years. The mill itself was a small, one-story stone affair with a sagging roof and broken windows. It did not take the girls long to determine that the Countess was not inside or anywhere around the place.

That left two houses along the road, both of which were deserted.

"I wonder why no one ever moved back into the houses on this road," Lenora murmured. "Of course the ground isn't very good for farming, and since the creek has dried up—"

"They are probably the reasons," Beverly smiled. "Let's leave the car here and walk."

The first house was beyond hope of occupancy and the girls did not have to search long to convince themselves that the Countess was not there.

"The last one," Lenora said, viewing the one remaining house.

From where the girls stood they could just see the green roof and brick chimney rising above a sudden dip in the road.

"This is our last chance. She must be there," Beverly said. "Lenora, go back to the police and tell them we followed the Countess this far. I have a hunch that she is in that house and that Larson is, too."

"And Kay?" Lenora murmured

"Yes," Beverly said solemnly. "Take the car and hurry. I'll stay here and see what I can learn."

"Not alone!" Lenora said. "Beverly, you won't go into that house without me!"

Beverly laughed. "Go along with you! The sooner you bring the police the sooner everything will be over."

"Beverly, I don't like it."

"Neither do I," Beverly said.

"Why don't you go for the police and let me stay here?" Lenora proposed. "I can report all that I see when you come back."

"Because you don't know what Larson looks like and I do," Beverly said. "You wouldn't know him if you saw him come out. He is the important one to find," she added grimly.

Beverly watched Lenora walk back to the old mill and a moment later her car sped down the road. Then Beverly turned her attention to the house ahead of her. She tried to shake off the feeling of uneasiness and loneliness that seemed to sweep down upon her now that Lenora had left her. It was foolish, she told herself. There was nothing wrong—yet.

She left the road and walked across the field, thinking

to come upon the house from the side. There was no use advertising the fact that the Countess had been followed to this house, if this is where she was.

The scraggly grass scratched and clung to her as she walked over the uneven ground. Deserted furrows, made years ago by industrious farmers, had left the field full of ruts, and she stumbled several times. A rabbit darted across her path, his white, powder-puff tail disappearing hastily in the grass. Beverly's heart raced and she stood still to take a deep breath. She could not have been more startled if an elephant had suddenly walked across her path—an elephant or Larson. Just the thought of Larson, his bearded face and his thick glasses with his small ferret eyes behind them, gave her cold shivers.

"Are you going to stand here all night?" she chided herself.

The afternoon was almost spent, and the cool, mellow twilight of the summer evening was about to descend on the world. Across the countryside came the sound of a church bell, the twittering of birds, and the lonely barking of a dog.

Beverly approached the rise of ground which hid the house and stopped to look down on the building. A green gabled roof, with a brick chimney sticking up through it like a finger pointing to the sky, surmounted the dirty brick walls of the house. The windows stared like empty eyes into the bare, flowerless garden bed. A broken fence surrounded the yard. There was no sign of life anywhere.

"The end of the trail."

Why did that phrase insist on haunting her? The house before her looked like the end of something, all right! Had the Countess gone in there? If so, why was there no sign of life? Why had the Countess come to such a deserted place to begin with? The answer, Beverly argued, could mean only one thing: Larson. They had worked together against Kresloff. Now they would elude the police together.

How about Kay? That was another anxious thought. What had happened to her? Was she, too, in that old house?

Beverly looked back the way she had come. If only Lenora would hurry! Meanwhile it was growing darker. The darkness would be both a blessing and a hindrance. She would not be able to see what went on about the house. If anyone was in the house, he would not be able to see her either.

Suppose Larson was in there. Suppose he saw the police charging down upon him. What would happen to Kay? He would not submit easily, and she would be the only weapon he could use against the police. Kay would be his shield, and Beverly hated to think what that might mean.

"You're guessing, Beverly," she told herself. "You're guessing that the Countess went into that house. You are guessing that Larson is there."

It was true. How did she know what the thick brick walls hid? She had to be sure the Countess was in there with Larson. Lenora might be bringing the police out here on a wild-goose chase. There was only one way to be sure. She must go down to the house and see if it was as deserted as it looked.

## CHAPTER XIV

## *Trapped*

---

THE wind that had started as a gentle whisper among the trees grew in volume until it swept leaves and dust before it in an angry cloud and rattled the windows and doors of the old house. Clouds quickly gathered overhead, and in the protection of the darkness, Beverly mounted the steps of the porch and paused at a window. Now, whether or not she wanted to go inside, she would have to seek protection from the storm.

She could see nothing on the other side of the window but an empty room with faded wallpaper and a long crack in the ceiling. She moved to the front door and took hold of the rusty latch, but the door would not open. Whether it was locked or merely stuck from disuse, she could not tell. She went back to the window but that, too, was shut tight and no amount of trying could budge it.

Thunder rumbled overhead and low on the horizon was a brilliant flash of lightning. The rain would come in a few minutes and unless she got inside, she would be soaked, for the roof over the porch was full of holes and offered no protection.

Cautiously she stepped down from the porch and walked along the side of the house, stopping to peer through each window and, when she saw no one, tried to open one of them. At last she came to a small cellar window in the back of the house. A little force broke the lock and cautiously she climbed in, feet first. It was dark and dirty inside. A cobweb brushed against her face as she moved toward the stairs she could see in the far corner. The light was dim now and fading swiftly. The cellar stairs were steep and narrow and, in places, rotted and full of splinters. It must have been a long time since anyone had gone up or down the stairs, for dust lay thick upon them and her footprints were plainly visible.

She heard the rain start and was glad. The sound of the raindrops would serve to hide, somewhat, the creaking of the steps beneath her weight. Cautiously she crept upward, upward into close, dusty darkness. The door at the head of the stairs stood ajar and she slid through the narrow opening into the empty kitchen. There was just enough dim gray light to see that there was no one else in the room.

Beverly crept from room to room cautiously, so noiselessly she might have been a ghost herself. There was nothing—nothing but the sound of the wind and the rain as it swept against the walls of the house. At last she stood at the window of the front room on the second floor and looked toward the road. At this point she would be able to see the headlights of a car as it came around the bend in the road. She felt puzzled and defeated. The Countess could not have come into this house. What had happened to the woman? Beverly thought again of the empty road. There had been no other place to go, yet she, Beverly, had just proved there was no one in the house. She had gone carefully from room to room and each one had been empty and silent beneath a blanket of dust.

She rested her forehead against the cool windowpane

and stared into the rain. It was too dark to see clearly, except when the flashes of lightning came. Then for an instant the world was brilliantly lighted.

What had happened to the Countess? The phrase repeated itself over and over again in her mind. Where had she disappeared so quickly? It was as if the earth had opened and swallowed her! And Beverly had been so sure she was close to finding both the Countess and Larson—as well as Kay Merrill!

It seemed like hours since she had sent Lenora for the police, but it really wasn't. It was the darkness of the summer storm that made it seem as if time had flown.

There was an old library table and a chair in the room in which she stood and she dragged the chair over to the window. As she did so there came a strange, uneven knocking. Lenora? At the door?

Beverly carefully retraced her steps to the staircase and groped her way down to the front door. She flung it open, but there was no one there. The wind flung the cold rain in her face and made it difficult to shut the door again. At last she leaned against it and strained her ears to hear the faintest sound.

What had made that knocking sound? The house was

empty—she had proven that to herself—and yet the shadows seemed full of strange, unknown elements. Ghosts? Nonsense, she told herself firmly. There are no such things as ghosts! It was most likely the wind.

She forced herself to go back up the stairs to the window where she could watch for Lenora, but it was not easy. She imagined eyes peering at her from dark corners, voices whispering, and formless figures moving in the shadows. Every creaky board she stepped upon was like a ghostly footstep behind her.

"Stop it!" she said aloud to herself. "Keep your imagination for your writing."

Her voice echoed eerily through the empty rooms, but it broke the silence and cheered her somewhat. She went back to the chair at the window and tried to think of something pleasant.

She would go home to Renville for a visit, when all this was over. Perhaps she and Shirley could take a trip somewhere this summer. She longed to return again to the mountains she had seen on her trip West. Snow-capped giants plucking at the blue sky, they were symbols of peace and everlasting beauty in the uncertain, changing world. She wanted to see them again. She wanted to follow a narrow mountain trail through fields of wild flowers and thick, pine-scented woods. She wanted to race her horse across a flat, dusty plateau, and splash with him across a cold, swift-rushing mountain stream. She wanted to get away from mystery and deception and old empty houses.

Beverly leaped to her feet and stood trembling, listening, fighting the desire to run and scream. A crash, close and deafening, had abruptly shaken her from her reverie and brought her back to the present. Had it been thunder? No. It had been different than the crash of thunder. It had seemed as though the very roof was about to crash down about her. No ghost ever made a noise like that!

Uneasily she looked about the room as it was lighted by a sudden, almost blinding flash of lightning. Tensely she waited for another flash. When it came she dropped to her knees on the dusty floor. Footprints! Dozens of them! She had not made them all, and in the darkness she had not noticed them before. Now they seemed to have a strange significance. Perhaps they held the answer to that mysterious knocking and to the awful crash she had just heard.

As the storm raged outside, the lightning flashes gave

Beverly enough light to see the footprints, to see that they were newly made. The dust had not settled into them yet. She followed the prints to a corner of the room and stopped. The footprints ended abruptly, close to the wall. She thought of ghosts and sliding panels. Ghosts did not make footprints in the first place, and the wall did not seem hollow enough to be hiding another room behind it. What, then, was the explanation? Footsteps did not just lead to a certain point and stop. There must be something beyond.

Again there came a loud crash overhead, followed by a thump—like a body falling, Beverly thought instinctively and shivered. She thought she heard, too, the faint murmur of voices. Of course it could be the wind banging something upon the roof and whispering in the eaves.

The next time the lightning came she looked up at the ceiling and there it was, a trap door set in one corner of the room. She had overlooked the attic hidden in the gabled roof! Was the Countess up there? Or was it her imagination playing tricks?

Beverly dragged the table beneath the trap door and placed the chair upon it. Then she climbed up and placed her ear against the trap door. All was silent. She pushed on it lightly and as it seemed to move, she pushed harder, raising it above her head, until she stood head and shoulders through the opening, staring into blackness.

There was a sudden scraping sound and then the round yellow beam of a flashlight shone straight into her eyes, blinding her.

"Welcome to our party, Miss Gray."

The voice was one she recognized with a rush of cold terror. Larson! She tried to withdraw but it was too late. Someone prodded her shoulder with something cold and hard and the chemistry professor pulled her up into the attic. She could not face him upright, the roof was too low for anyone to stand straight, so she half crouched while she waited for him to make the first move.

A match flickered at one end of the room and the Countess applied it to a candle. Over the flame she smiled at Beverly.

"So you did come into this house!" Beverly exclaimed.

"It took you a long while to find me," the Countess replied.

"You would have gone away again if it had not been for her," Larson said disgustedly, jerking his head toward the wall.

Beverly looked over to see Kay Merrill lying on the floor, her eyes closed.

"What happened?" Beverly asked, her heart contracting with fear.

"She tried to warn you," Larson said. "She ran to the trap door but stumbled and hit her head. If she had remained silent as we told her it would not have happened. You would have given up the search and gone away without finding us."

"And you might have escaped," Beverly murmured.

"Your friend—where is she?" The Countess brought the candle close to Beverly. "Two of you followed me. Where is the other girl?"

"Answer!" Larson commanded, shaking Beverly's arm when she was silent.

"She will be here any minute," Beverly said.

"With the police, no doubt!" Larson exclaimed.

He pushed Beverly aside and leaned forward to blow out the candle. Then he hurried to the front of the house to peer out into the rain.

Beverly knelt beside Kay Merrill and lifted the other girl's head to her lap.

"Kay! Kay!" she said urgently.

"Oooo!" the *Sun* reporter stirred slowly.

"Lie still," Beverly cautioned in a whisper.

"Who—who is it?" Kay struggled to a sitting position. "Beverly—is that you?"

"Yes," Beverly murmured. "How do you feel?"

"As if there were millions of tiny men with hammers inside my head," Kay groaned. "Beverly Gray, how did they get you? I tried to warn you—"

"I know," Beverly said, "but I didn't realize that until too late."

"They said they would kill me if I made any noise," Kay continued. "Beverly—what are we going to do?"

"Lenora has gone for the police," Beverly whispered. "That is our only hope."

"That makes me feel a little better," Kay said. She dropped her head into her hands.

"Has it been a terrible time, Kay?" Beverly asked gently.

"Not really," Kay said. "He brought me here yesterday as a hostage. He didn't do anything but look out the window until the woman came." Kay moved closer to Beverly. "What is it all about, Beverly? Did they catch Kresloff?"

"Yes," Beverly said. "They have him and his formula, but Larson and the Countess are responsible for the wrecking of the mail plane. Too, Larson may have a copy of the explosive formula because he was working with Kresloff."

When Beverly finished telling Kay all that had happened, the *Sun* reporter chuckled.

"It looks as though I'll be in on the end of the story after all."

"Now I know you are feeling better," Beverly declared. "Is there any way out of this attic, Kay, other than the trap door?"

Kay shook her head. "There is only one small window at the front. I tried my best to fine some other means of escape last night."

"Then we must wait for Lenora," Beverly said, settling back against the wall.

She felt tired and the room was hot. The staccato beat of the rain on the roof was close over their heads, a monotonous rhythm. There was no sound from Larson at the small window. The Countess was somewhere at the other end of the room and Beverly surmised she was standing guard over the trap door.

Suddenly there was a low exclamation, like a long-drawn-out sigh, from Larson. It brought both Kay and Beverly to attention. Faintly they heard the hum of an automobile motor as a car struggled over the muddy road.

"Beverly!" In the darkness Kay's hand grasped Beverly's arm tightly.

"I hear it," Beverly nodded. "It must be Lenora and the police."

The Countess and Larson approached the girls. The Countess lighted her candle and the flickering light made huge, grotesque shadows on the wall.

"You will be silent if anyone enters the house," Larson commanded the girls.

"I shall scream as loudly as I can," Kay retorted spiritedly.

"That will be most unfortunate," Larson declared. The cold steel of a revolver appeared in his hand. "I am prepared for anything, you see. I have nothing to lose."

"Nor I," smiled the Countess.

"What a story this will make!" Kay breathed.

"It is unfortunate you let enthusiasm for your position lead you into such a situation as this," Larson declared. "It is too bad you shall not be able to write your story."

"A good reporter doesn't give up until the end of the story is reached," Kay smiled. "It isn't finished yet."

The sound of the automobile motor had stopped now, and faintly there came to those listening the murmur of voices as the new arrivals entered the house.

"Remember! Silence!"

Beverly looked at the grim-faced man before them, at the evil-looking gun in his hand, at the Countess standing tense and silent, and, lastly, at the white, strained face of the girl beside her. Kay had been through a lot and she had about reached the end of her endurance, but her pride kept her from admitting it.

A few months ago she and Kay were enemies, working for rival newspapers. It was odd how circumstances could make friends of people. Here, in danger, she and Kay were allies, and Beverly knew that they would be friends ever afterward. They would take from this adventure together a new respect and a new understanding of each other.

"If one of you screams, I shall shoot the other," Larson muttered grimly.

He was a desperate man and ready to take desperate

measures. He had to do something to enforce their obedience and this was it. If one girl should be heroic and want to scream, without regard to the consequences to herself, she would quell that desire because it would bring harm to her companion. Beverly knew very well she would not scream and thus cause Larson to shoot Kay!

"Smart, aren't you?" Kay muttered, and Beverly knew she had been thinking the same thing.

Kay looked at Beverly silently and her eyes seemed to plead with Beverly to think of something—of some way out of their predicament.

Voices and footsteps rose faintly from the house below them. Lenora and the police were searching for them—searching the house room by room, as Beverly had done, and finding nothing. The voices grew in volume until the four in the attic knew the new arrivals stood right beneath them. Hope flamed anew. If only someone would look up at the ceiling and see the trap door! If it were possible to transmit thought through space to another individual, surely Lenora must feel something!

"Bev—er—leee!" Lenora's voice rose in a call that penetrated to the very rafters.

Below them, so close and yet so far, was rescue for themselves and doom for Larson and the Countess. Weeks of patient work had led Beverly to this spot. Were all her efforts going to be wasted? Hopelessly she looked at the other girl.

Kay opened her mouth to speak and Larson brought his gun up sharply until the little round barrel was pointed directly at Beverly, so Kay remained silent.

The candle flickered in the Countess' hand. Melted wax dripped on the floor. Seconds seemed years long. Gradually the voices below them died away. Beverly's heart sank. Lenora was leaving.

"Beverly!" Kay whispered despairingly.

"Silence!" Larson hissed.

It was like an old-fashioned melodrama, Beverly thought—the villain and his accomplice, and the two helpless victims. It did not seem possible that such a thing was happening—not today, not in the twentieth century!

There was the sound of a motor starting outside and the slamming of automobile doors. Larson relaxed with an infuriating smirk. He tiptoed to the window and peeped out. Then, oddly enough, the engine stopped and running footsteps sounded again on the porch. Someone was returning. The girls were being given a second chance!

"This is it!" Beverly murmured to Kay. "It is now or never."

"Right-o!" Kay sang out.

Empty, forgotten boxes had been flung in the attic at different times by the former occupants of the house. They had remained through the years and now Kay put her hands against a pile of them and pushed with all her might. The boxes toppled and fell with a loud, splintering crash. The top box hit the Countess, knocking the candle from her hand. She screamed shrilly and shrank back against the wall as a second column of boxes came tumbling down.

"I forgot she was the screaming type," Beverly laughed. "Lenora should have heard that."

Meanwhile, Larson came running back from the window. He shouted hoarse commands, to which the girls paid no heed. A shot rang out in the darkness and both Kay and Beverly promptly dropped flat on the floor. Now that the candle was out, the room was in utter blackness and he could not take careful aim with his gun. The girls could hear him stumbling about, muttering savagely. Then he struck a match and held it above his head. For a few seconds it gave a weak, flickering light, then it died away.

Shouts were heard now from the lower part of the house and heavy footsteps raced from the first to second floors.

"Lenora!" Beverly shouted as loudly as she could.

Her voice revealed her position to Larson and a bullet buried itself in the wall above her head. Kay had found a short, heavy stick and she rapped heavily on the floor with it.

Larson turned his attention to something else. In the darkness the girls could not make out what he was doing until the Countess moved to help him and they heard the boxes being dragged across the floor.

"He is barricading the trap door!" Beverly exclaimed.

"They'll never get in to us," Kay muttered. "What'll we do?"

"The window!" Beverly whispered. "Come on!"

They groped their way to the other end of the room. A blow from the stick Kay held tore aside the shade that had been tacked over the window, but no amount of strength could open the window. Kay shattered the pane with her stick and leaned out.

"Help!" she shrieked.

"How do we get up there?" A man's voice rose out of the darkness below.

"A trap door—" Kay was beginning when a heavy hand dragged her back and Larson bent forward to shoot once out the window.

Someone pounded heavily on the trap door and the boxes which had been piled upon it wobbled dangerously. Larson darted back toward the corner and helped the Countess pile another heavy box over the door.

"Kay," Beverly whispered hastily, "do you know anything about firearms?"

"A little. I used to go hunting with my father."

"How many bullets does the revolver he has hold?"

"Six. Why?"

"He has already fired three," Beverly murmured.

"I see what you mean!" Kay exclaimed. "If we can make him use the other three bullets he won't have a weapon!"

"We'll have a good chance then," Beverly agreed.

"What can we do?" Kay pondered. "I know!"

Quickly and expertly she threw the stick she held. It landed with a clatter in the far corner of the room. Larson whirled and shot blindly at the noise.

"Only two left!" Kay murmured gleefully. "This is like the game 'Ten Little Indians.'"

"Beverly!" Lenora's voice came through the broken window. "Beverly!"

"Here!" Beverly replied, leaning out the narrow opening.

"Are you all right?" Lenora cried.

"Why don't you hurry?" Kay shouted over Beverly's shoulder.

"The trap door is stuck," Lenora returned. "Is the Countess up there with you?"

"And Larson," Beverly called back.

At the sound of his name Larson came charging down the room like an angry bull. He pushed the girls aside and furiously fired his gun twice through the open window. Gone was the suave chemistry professor, and the man in his place was like a trapped, savage animal.

"You might as well give up," Beverly declared. "You cannot fight forever."

"They will never take me!" Larson screamed at them.

"I have worked years on my experiments, and I must have time to finish. They cannot take me to prison!"

"You have no way of escaping," Kay Merrill retorted. "The house is surrounded. Your gun is empty. You have nothing to fight with."

The man made no reply. Instead he hurried back to the Countess and together they held the boxes over the trap door. Kay began groping around in the darkness on the floor.

"What are you looking for?" Beverly asked.

"The candle," Kay said. "I have an inspiration. Ah! Here it is!"

"What are you going to do?"

"I've heard of hunters smoking out wild animals. Maybe we can smoke out Larson," Kay said, producing matches and striking a flame.

"You don't propose to burn the house down, do you?" Beverly demanded.

"No," Kay replied with a low chuckle.

Beverly followed closely behind Kay as she walked toward Larson and the Countess. The candle flickered smokily. What Kay proposed to do was not exactly clear to Beverly, but she welcomed action of any sort.

The efforts of their rescuers seemed to have stopped and all was silent. Beverly supposed they were considering the situation, gathering their forces for a final blow. Even the wind and the rain had stopped. It was as if the world waited and watched the drama being played here in the attic of the old house.

The candle clearly revealed Larson's dark face with the thick beard and blazing eyes.

"Go back and sit down in the corner," Larson commanded.

"Why don't you give up?" Kay retorted.

"You should never have brought her to this place!" the Countess flared at Larson about Kay.

"She followed me," he retorted, "and all would have been well—they would not have found me if you had not come and brought another reporter!"

While the two fugitives snarled at each other Kay moved closer.

"If you don't open the door this minute I shall drop this candle into that box of sawdust. You know what would happen!"

"You wouldn't dare!" the Countess gasped. "It would burn the house!"

"In an instant this whole room would be ablaze," Kay nodded.

Beverly felt her heart leap as she looked at the other girl's pale face. The flickering candlelight cast dark shadows beneath Kay's eyes and gave her a queer, ghostly appearance.

"Even I don't know if she really means it!" Beverly thought with a shock.

Kay had been her rival—an implacable rival for headlines. What did Beverly really know of her? Perhaps Kay was dazed with her recent experiences. Perhaps she did not fully realize what she was saying.

Beverly could see her own doubts mirrored in the eyes of the Countess. Even Larson looked dazed at the sudden turn of events.

"Start moving the boxes, Beverly," Kay said over her shoulder.

Beverly stepped forward and began pushing the boxes aside. At the same instant, activity began below them, indicating that at the first opportunity the police would be up through the opening.

With a cry of outrage Larson leaped swiftly toward the candle in Kay's hand.

"Beverly!" Kay screamed.

Beverly pushed with all her might and a column of boxes tumbled down upon Larson's head. The Countess rushed to aid her cohort and that gave Kay and Beverly sufficient time to clear the trap door and let in their friends.

## CHAPTER XV

## *A New Arrival*

---

THE room was silent, each of its occupants intent on the newspaper in her hands, newspapers bearing the names of *Tribune* and *Sun*.

"It reads like a fairy tale," Lois declared at last, putting down her paper.

"In which the lovely princesses were rescued from the wicked dragon in the nick of time," added Lenora.

"It is the biggest story I ever wrote," Beverly declared. She stared at the picture on the front page of the paper in her hands. It was a good likeness of the Countess. "The end of the trail," she murmured.

"This is one story you and Kay Merrill had to share," Shirley smiled.

"I'd love to have seen Kay with that candle," Lenora said.

"She even had me wondering," Beverly laughed. "She looked as though she was ready to do anything."

"I never saw so much mud as there was that night," Lenora declared. "We were in a hurry to get to the house and the road was almost impassable. We got stuck I don't know how many times."

"It was a regular cloudburst," Beverly agreed.

"Did Lieutenant Petersen give you something else to work on?" Shirley asked Beverly.

Beverly shook her head. "No, thanks! I've been a spy for the last time!"

"Just like Mata Hari," Lois giggled.

"Jest if you must," Lenora interrupted loftily, "but I heard the Lieutenant thank Beverly for the splendid job she did."

"We know she did a splendid job," Shirley replied soberly. "I still shiver when I think of what might have happened."

"It is all over now," Beverly said. "Kresloff's discovery

is in safe hands where it will be used only for the good of society, and he and the Countess and Larson will be punished for the wreck of the mail plane and obtaining money under false pretenses."

"Everything ended happily," Lois sighed.

"Even Lenora got her picture of 'The Man Who Hates Cameras,'" Shirley said.

"I'll wager Beverly will be glad to get back to the nice quiet life on the *Tribune*," Lenora sighed.

"Quiet life!" Lois scoffed. "No Alpha Delta ever led a quiet life. I wonder what will happen next?"

"For the immediate present I suggest a nice long drive," Beverly smiled. "I must have your august approval of my new car. Ladies, the chariot awaits without—"

The newspapers were abandoned hastily and the girls trooped down to Beverly's car parked at the curb. After a brief discussion over who was to sit where, Shirley climbed in beside Beverly while Lenora and Lois shared the rumble seat.

The girls had dinner at a small country inn overlooking the Hudson and returned to town immediately afterward so that Shirley should not be late for her performance in *Angels Arise*. It was on the ride back to town, with the summer sunset lending a golden haze to the last hours before twilight, that Shirley made her proposal.

"Beverly, let's go somewhere—on a trip, I mean. The play closes tomorrow night and I'll be free. You need a vacation, too. After all, that adventure of yours wasn't any picnic! Let's take the car and drive and drive—"

"Believe it or not," Beverly smiled, "I was going to suggest the same thing to you. I was thinking of going West—"

"Mmm!" Shirley said happily. "That will be fun."

"You can't go without us," Lois shouted from the rear.

"Could you really go, Lois?" Lenora asked gleefully.

"My vacation is due any day," Lois nodded.

"The Four Musketeers!" Lenora misquoted with a grin. "It will be just like the days at Vernon."

Plans were made eagerly in the days that followed. Nearly every evening found road maps spread out upon the living room floor and the girls bent over them attentively. Then, one afternoon, Shirley came home with news.

"My uncle has died and left me his ranch."

"I hope it isn't like the house Phyllis inherited in

Maine," Lenora declared. "Remember that? It teemed with smugglers and stuff."

Shirley laughed. "I hardly think that is the case here. The place has been a cattle ranch for years. My uncle lived on it ever since he was a young man."

"Where is it?" Lois inquired.

"Montana."

"Shades of the Great Divide!" Lenora exclaimed. "Let's go. Now we have an objective for our trip."

"That is hundreds of miles away!" Lois said aghast.

"What of it?" Lenora shrugged.

"I would like to see it," Shirley murmured. "The pictures I have seen of it look grand."

"Cowboys and horses and things?" Lenora inquired eagerly.

"Rattlesnakes and bears and—" Lois began.

"Don't be so unromantic!" Lenora said sternly. "What do you think, Bev? After all, we are going in your car. Do we go to Montana?"

"I'd love it!" Beverly exclaimed. "Mountains and blue sky and wild flowers—"

"I can hardly wait," Lenora declared. "Now if Charlie Blaine will only be big-hearted and give me a vacation—

Maybe I can convince him the West has some good material for pictures," she added brightly. "It might be just the thing he is looking for to rival Kay's stories when she starts traveling around the country reporting from spots of historic interest!"

"It will be nice—" Shirley started to say when there was a knock on the door.

Lois, who was closest, opened it and took the cablegram Mrs. Callahan handed her.

"For Beverly," Lois said.

"Me?" Beverly exclaimed in surprise. Her first thought was for Larry, but then she recalled the letter she had received from him the day before had said he did not know exactly when he would be home.

She read the brief message and frowned thoughtfully. Then she read it again.

"What is it, Bev?" Shirley inquired. "Bad news?"

"Listen," Beverly said and read the message aloud. " 'Arrive New York tomorrow morning on S.S. Mermaid. Please meet boat. Signed, Cousin Harriet.' "

"Who in the world is Cousin Harriet?" Lois asked.

"I think I have a Cousin Harriet in England," Beverly murmured.

"You are about to have Cousin Harriet in New York," Lenora laughed.

"I've never seen her," Beverly continued thoughtfully. "I haven't the vaguest notion what she is like."

"It is odd she didn't let you know she was coming," Shirley commented. "Well, we'll have a welcoming dinner for her tomorrow night."

"I think I'll telephone my mother," Beverly said, "and learn something about Cousin Harriet."

All night long Beverly thought about the new arrival. What sort of a girl would her cousin be? Would she like the Alpha Deltas and would they like her? Would Harriet's arrival at this time interfere with the girls' proposed trip? Questions made her sleep light and restlessly, and at the breakfast table she invited Lenora to go to the boat with her. She felt she wanted to discuss Harriet with someone.

The girls walked out through the dark crowded pier to where the newest of ocean-going liners had just moored. The boat was like a majestic white gull poised for an instant on the gentle swell of water. Portholes were open to the sun. Brass fixtures shone brightly.

Lenora and Beverly went on board to find Harriet and

offer their assistance in getting her luggage through the customs and into Beverly's car. They made their way among the people on deck, noting the passengers, especially a tall blond girl, exquisitely dressed, standing by the rail facing a bevy of photographers.

"She is positively dripping with glamour," Lenora mused.

"Aren't you going to get her picture?" Beverly asked, indicating the camera which Lenora was never without on trips like this.

"No. Every paper in town will have it. The *Tribune* will be different. Come on, let's find your cousin."

They got the number of Harriet's stateroom from the purser, but upon reaching the room they found it empty, except for a neat pile of expensive luggage.

"Looks as though she intends to stay a while," Lenora declared, motioning toward the bags. "I don't think they will all fit into our closets."

A steward went down the corridor and Beverly called to him.

"Do you know whether Miss Fairchild has gone ashore?"

"I believe she is still on deck, Miss."

The girls returned to the crowded deck.

"If only I knew what she looked like," Beverly sighed, surveying the crowd of passengers lining the rail. There was a nice-looking girl standing to one side, winding her camera, and hopefully Beverly approached her.

"Pardon me, are you Miss Fairchild?"

"Oh, no," was the smiling answer. "That is Miss Fairchild." The girl nodded toward the stern where the tall blonde they had seen when they first came on board was being photographed against the skyline.

"You mean the glamour girl?" Lenora echoed in amazement.

"Well, well, Cousin Harriet!" Beverly murmured with a smile. The girl was not at all what she had expected. She looked at Lenora. "What shall we do with her?"

"I think I'll win her favor by taking her picture after all," Lenora replied. "It should make the society page on Sunday."

Harriet Fairchild was cheerfully willing to pose for a picture when Lenora revealed her press card and Beverly stood back, watching them. It seemed odd that she had never before seen her cousin. Why had Harriet chosen to come to New York now?

When Lenora had taken her picture, Beverly went forward and introduced herself. Harriet greeted her effusively.

"Dear Beverly!"

Beverly felt a little embarrassed. How could Harriet be so rapturous? After all, she was as much a stranger to Harriet as Harriet was to her.

Beverly introduced Lenora as a friend, not a reporter, and the three prepared to leave the ship. As they reached Beverly's car and began piling Harriet's luggage in the rumble seat the new arrival smiled.

"Isn't the car a little small, Beverly?"

"It's a fine car," Lenora returned.

"I'm sure it is," Harriet agreed, taking her place between Beverly and Lenora. "It is just—"

"What?" Beverly asked smilingly.

"You aren't what I expected, Beverly," was the candid reply. "I mean, a popular playwright—your books—"

"You aren't what I expected either," Beverly replied calmly, and she heard Lenora give a low chuckle.

When she thought of how she had pictured a timid, shy sort of person, instead of this smoothly dressed, modern girl, she felt like chuckling, too. She had thought how pleasant it would be to show a stranger around New York, revealing the wonders of the city. Somehow she did not think Harriet would be very impressed. Certainly New York would not overwhelm her!

"Our apartment isn't very large," Beverly told her cousin, "but we would love to have you stay with us while you are here."

"That is sweet of you, but I've already made reservations at the Saint James," her cousin answered.

"The Saint James!" Lenora exclaimed. It was the most expensive of the large hotels.

"Yes. It is a good one, isn't it?" Harriet asked. "It was recommended to me by a friend."

"It is a fine hotel," Lenora agreed.

They drove Harriet to her hotel and went up to her suite with her. There was a large sitting room, tastefully furnished, and beyond that a huge bedroom with windows that commanded an excellent view of the city, and a green and white tile bath.

Harriet said she would be tired when she finished unpacking and she would rest during the afternoon, but that she would love to have dinner with them, so the girls left her alone.

"Somehow I don't think Cousin Harriet would appreciate the chummy dinner we planned at the apartment for tonight," Beverly said as the girls went down in the elevator.

"Somehow, I agree with you," Lenora laughed. "She is something special, isn't she?"

"Suppose we take her to the new Mirror Room?" Beverly suggested. "It will be my party. I'd like to give Shirley a celebration, too, upon the closing of the play."

"If it takes us to the Mirror Room, I say hurrah for Cousin Harriet!" Lenora teased. "Now I'm off. I have to take some pictures of a society luncheon at the Warwick and Charlie Blaine told me not to be late. I'll see you tonight."

Beverly went home to the apartment and got busy arranging for her dinner party. She made her reservation at the Mirror Room and then telephoned Jim Stanton and asked him to get in touch with Roger and Paul and one or two other young men whom the girls had met since living in New York. If only Larry were here, the evening would be complete. It seemed years since she had seen him off on the plane. His letters were frequent and newsy, but of course they could not make up for his absence.

Meantime, Lenora had completed her assignment and had gone back to the *Tribune* office. She took her pictures to the darkroom and waited the developments with interest. One of the first to come through was the one she had taken of Harriet on the boat. She was standing at the window looking at the picture when another *Tribune* photographer stopped to admire it.

"A good picture," he commented. "Who is the girl?"

"Cousin of a friend of mine," Lenora replied.

"She looks familiar," the man continued. "I've seen her somewhere before."

"That isn't likely," Lenora smiled. "She just got off the boat from England this morning for her first visit in New York."

"I still think she looks familiar," he insisted. "I believe I took her picture once. Is she famous for anything?"

"Not that I know of," Lenora replied. "She might look like someone else you know."

The man took the picture from Lenora's hand and looked at it more closely.

"I'm not mistaken," he declared. "I've seen her before."

"If you took her picture it should be in the *Tribune's* files," Lenora murmured. If the man was right and he had seen the girl before, what did it mean? Harriet herself had said this was her first visit to New York.

"It has been within the past year," Lenora's companion stated firmly. "Yes, sir! I've seen this girl before."

"You interest me," Lenora laughed. "Do you suppose I could go through the files and see if I can find the picture you took?"

"I'll help you," the man offered. "I'm interested, too." For two hours Lenora and her companion leafed through photographs taken for the *Tribune* over a period of twelve months.

"Here it is!" The man triumphantly whipped from the files a black and white print of a girl in a bathing suit. "She was one of the runner-ups in last year's contest for Miss New York."

"Imagine that!" Lenora whistled. Then her eyes grew thoughtful. A New York girl claiming to be Beverly's cousin from England. What did it mean? Lenora determined to find out.

"Don't tell anyone about this," she murmured to the

other photographer. "I want to surprise some one."

"Okay!"

He went away whistling and Lenora carefully put the picture back in the file.

Dear Cousin Harriet! A fraud! Lenora was busy thinking as she went home to dress for the dinner party. Should she reveal Harriet's true identity at once, or should she bide her time and try to determine why, out of all the people in New York, the girl should pick Beverly as her cousin? Did she plan something harmful to Beverly? Lenora decided on a course of watchful waiting. She would become a devoted friend of Harriet's and learn what was at the bottom of the deception.

The dinner party started brilliantly. Beverly and Jim and a boy with whom Jim worked, Lou Travers, called for Harriet at her hotel. She was wearing a black lace gown that made her blond beauty seem even more gold and glowing. Both Jim and Lou were impressed with the beauty of Beverly's cousin and everyone was in high spirits when they joined the rest of their party in the Mirror Room. The room was lighted softly, with tints that flattered the gay colors of the girls' gowns. The music was just the right tempo and tone, and the dinner was excellent, when they remembered to stop dancing long enough to eat it.

"I have never had such a gay time," Harriet declared to Beverly close to the end of the evening. "It was sweet of you to arrange the party for me."

"It is partly for Shirley, too," Beverly confessed. "She did such a magnificent job in *Angels Arise*—"

"Ah, yes, that was your play, wasn't it?" Harriet murmured. "I would love to see it."

"It is closed for the summer," Beverly told her, "but Shirley will open in it again in September. If you are here then—"

"I may be," Harriet murmured. "Is Shirley a very good actress?"

"Excellent!" Beverly declared.

'She is lucky to have you to write plays for her," Harriet continued. "I wish you would write one for me some day."

"I didn't know you were an actress," Beverly said in surprise.

"I'm not," Harriet confessed. "Not yet."

The last two words were so low that Lenora, who sat on the other side of Harriet and who had silently listened to the conversation, was sure she was the only one who had heard them.

Jim brought Shirley back to the table and asked Harriet to dance. Lenora took the opportunity to slide into the seat beside Beverly.

"Harriet is beautiful, isn't she, Bev?"

Beverly nodded.

"Isn't it strange that she should have theatrical aspirations, too?" Lenora continued.

"I don't think so," Beverly replied. "There are a lot of girls who would like to be actresses. Don't you have a secret ambition?" she asked teasingly.

Lenora responded with a chuckle. "It has always been my secret desire to ride a fire engine—in the seat at the end of the long ladder, but I'm afraid nothing will ever come of it."

"Probably nothing will ever come of Harriet's desire, either," Beverly smiled. "She doesn't seem to me to be the dramatic type."

Yet she is acting now, Lenora thought. She is acting every minute she poses as Beverly's cousin. She does it so convincingly, too. She is either an excellent actress or really Beverly's cousin. Was it possible that there were two people—one in England and one in New York—who looked so much alike they could be mistaken for each other? "Go slowly!" Lenora warned herself. If she falsely accused Harriet, someone might be hurt.

"Are you sure she has never been in New York before?" Lenora asked Beverly with a frown. "She doesn't seem at all strange to this."

"Well, after all," Beverly laughed, "England isn't a wilderness!"

"No," Lenora agreed, and said no more on the subject. It was obvious that Beverly had accepted the girl for what she claimed to be. Could she, Lenora, be mistaken? Still, there was that photograph—

The evening was a huge success. Everyone declared it was the happiest time he had ever had, and it was very late when the four Alpha Delta girls returned to their apartment.

"Is Lenora going to sit up all night?" Lois inquired with a yawn as she climbed into bed.

"I'll see what's the matter," Beverly volunteered.

She went out to the living room where she found Lenora standing at the window staring at the moonlit street below.

"What's up, chum?" Beverly asked, slipping an arm about her friend. "Are you sick?"

"No," Lenora shook her head and sat down on the window seat.

"Cry on my shoulder if you want to," Beverly invited. "What's wrong?"

"I've been thinking," Lenora replied. "Beverly, if you suspected something about someone, and even though everyone else thought this person was all right, would you follow your own convictions?"

"What someone?" Beverly inquired.

Lenora shook her head. "I can't tell you. I just have a feeling about—something."

" 'To thine own self be true—' " Beverly quoted softly. "We learned that in school, remember? It is good advice, too. Can I help you, Lenora?"

"No," Lenora said. "Beverly—this thing I suspect—it isn't very pleasant, but something must be done and I'm the only one—"

"Do what you think is best," Beverly counseled. "If your course is straight and true, you'll weather the storm. Now go to bed and forget your troubles for tonight."

Lenora went into the bedroom and Beverly turned out

the lights. Moonlight made a silver path on the floor and she knelt on the window seat to lift her eyes to the stars. She would never have suspected Lenora of having secret worries. The blond girl was always so cheerful, so full of fun. It was odd that no matter how close you felt to a person, you could never really know what went on inside of her until it was put into words. Take Harriet, for example. Her cousin seemed a charming girl, beautiful and friendly. Yet sometimes, in unguarded moments, there was a shadow in her eyes. Sometimes her laughter did not ring true. "Oh, well!" Beverly sighed. Perhaps when she got to know Harriet better her cousin would reveal what was bothering her.

The next day, when she knew Beverly had gone to get a story on the launching of a new ocean liner, Lenora telephoned Harriet and invited her to lunch. She asked a great many questions and to all of them Harriet gave fairly satisfactory answers. Still Lenora's doubts persisted. She told herself Harriet did not have a true British accent. Her clothes, too, looked as though they had come from New York and not London shops. By the time Lenora said good-by to Harriet she was more bewildered than ever.

A concert had been selected for that evening and before it they had dinner at Smitty's. There was nothing formal about it. It was just a group of girls together having fun, and Harriet seemed to enjoy it as much as the Mirror Room.

"I can't figure her out," Lenora sighed when she and Lois were alone in the kitchen after their return from the concert.

"Harriet?" Lois inquired. "I think she is charming."

"That's it!" Lenora agreed. "She enters into our fun, she talks to us, laughs with us, seems to enjoy our company and all the while she—"

"What?"

"Oh—nothing!"

Lenora had been about to say that despite all those things Harriet was fooling them all. But how could she be sure? Perhaps it was silly to let her imagination run away like this. She would give up the whole idea and accept Harriet for what she seemed to be.

That resolution lasted for one whole day. Then her doubts began to creep back again, especially after she saw Harriet lunching with a man in a restaurant on Broadway. The man was a stranger and Lenora wondered where she had met him. Harriet had said she knew no one in the city but the girls.

Lenora waited on the pavement until Harriet and her companion left the restaurant. As they waited to cross the street, Lenora took careful aim with her camera and caught a good likeness of them both. Later, when the picture was developed, she took it to the photographer who had first claimed to recognize Harriet.

"Fred, do you know this man?"

Fred nodded. "He is a publicity man. Why?"

"Publicity!" Lenora echoed. "I wonder what he was doing with Harriet?"

"If she wants to go on the stage he is probably trying to get her a job," Fred returned.

Lenora remembered only too well the desire to be an actress which Harriet had confessed that first evening in the Mirror Room, but would anyone go to such lengths to secure a place in the theater? What did she hope to gain by posing as Beverly's cousin? Beverly wrote plays, she did not produce them.

There was one way to settle all this and Lenora decided to do it. Perhaps it was a lot to take upon herself, but she wanted to be sure—for Beverly's sake—before she exposed Harriet. That afternoon she sent a long cable-gram and tried to wait patiently for a reply.

The girls got together again that evening and went swimming in the Y.W.C.A. pool. For a few minutes Lenora and Harriet were alone at the edge of the pool, watching Lois dive from the springboard.

"What do you think of your cousin?" Lenora asked, watching the other girl closely.

"Beverly? I like her very much," Harriet said promptly. "I only wish—"

"What?"

"Nothing. I like all you girls," Harriet continued, pulling on her bathing cap. "You've all been very nice to me. I wish there were some way in which I could repay you."

"You can," Lenora said promptly.

"How?"

"Well, I wouldn't want to see Beverly hurt by anyone," Lenora stated calmly.

Harriet's eyes met hers and Lenora knew, in that minute, that Harriet was no more Beverly's cousin than she was, but how would she prove it?

"Neither would I," Harriet said at last, and dove into

the water without giving Lenora an opportunity to continue the conversation.

The reply to Lenora's cablegram came the next day. It stated very plainly that Harriet Fairchild was still in London. Anyone using that name was an impostor. Grimly determined, the cable in her pocket, Lenora went to the Saint James Hotel, but Harriet was not in her room. Lenora had to go home with her fury unspent.

Lenora had scarcely taken off her hat when Shirley swept in and slammed the door behind her so viciously the pictures on the wall shook.

"What-ho!" Lenora said in surprise. "What is bothering you?"

"Where is Beverly?" Shirley demanded.

"I haven't seen her since early this morning," Lenora replied. "Sit down. Hot, isn't it? I hope Lois gets her vacation soon so we can take our trip and escape this heat."

Shirley dropped into a chair and stared at her friend.

"Lenora, be honest with me. Do you think I was any good in *Angels Arise?*"

"It was the best performance I ever saw," Lenora said simply.

"Are you saying that just because I am one of the Alpha Deltas?" Shirley persisted.

"You know Dale Arden is a good actress," Lenora returned. "What is all this?"

Shirley got up to pace nervously up and down the room. "If I was good, why did Beverly ask to have someone else in the play next year?"

"Beverly asked that?" Lenora demanded aghast. "I don't believe it!"

"I didn't either—at first," Shirley sighed.

"Tell me what happened," Lenora commanded.

"I met the producer of *Angels Arise* on the street," Shirley told her. "He seemed very upset. He didn't really want to tell me, but I asked him something about the play and the whole thing tumbled out. It seems Beverly sent her cousin to see him and ask that he send the play on tour this summer with Harriet in the lead instead of me. That would put her in the lead when it opens here again in September."

"Harriet!" Lenora jumped up. "Then this is what she has been working for!"

"I didn't think Beverly would do anything like that without telling me first," Shirley continued in a worried tone. "I wonder what she didn't like about the way I played the part? I tried to do everything the way she and I had discussed it—"

"Believe me," Lenora said excitedly, "Beverly loved the way you played the part. Harriet! Dear Cousin Harriet! Oh, boy! There are going to be fireworks now!"

"What are you talking about?" Shirley asked.

"Harriet!" Lenora said excitedly. "I have a choice bit of news for you. Harriet isn't—"

"Hi, gals!" Beverly came in and dropped into a chair. "Isn't it hot today!"

"Why didn't you tell me you wanted someone else to play the lead in *Angels Arise* when it opens in September?" Shirley demanded stormily at once.

Beverly looked at her in bewilderment. "But I don't."

"I heard differently," Shirley said, her face flaming. "I don't think it was very sporting of you to have Harriet take the message to the producer. You might have told me yourself—"

"Wait a minute!" Beverly exclaimed sharply. "What does Harriet have to do with this?"

"You should know since you want her to play the lead," Shirley retorted angrily.

"Shirley, please!" Beverly said. "I've just discovered something."

"So have I," Lenora interrupted. "Harriet isn't your cousin, Bev."

"I know," Beverly said. "I learned it this morning. My mother had a letter from England and she telephoned me. Harriet is working in London. This girl is an impostor. I tried to reach her at her hotel to talk to her but she wasn't in."

"I tried to talk to her, too," Lenora murmured.

"How did you learn it?" Beverly asked.

Lenora proceeded to tell them of her suspicions and her confirmation while Shirley regarded them both wide-eyed.

"Lois was right when she said an Alpha Delta never leads a quiet life!" Beverly declared. "I'm going to telephone the Saint James and see if she has come in yet. The very idea! Posing as my cousin—"

At that moment there was a timid knock on the door and when Beverly threw it open they all were amazed to see Harriet on the threshold.

"May I come in?" she asked quietly. "I want to talk to you."

"We want to talk to you, too," Beverly said promptly.

"May I say what I have to say first?" Harriet asked. "Otherwise, I may lose my courage."

"Go ahead," Beverly invited.

Harriet stood in the center of the room, twisting a handkerchief nervously in her hands.

"I've been walking all day, trying to make up my mind to come here to tell you."

"Tell us what?" Lenora prodded.

"That I am not really Beverly's cousin. It was all a publicity stunt," the girl blurted out. "It seemed like a good idea at first, but you were all so nice to me I just couldn't go through with it."

"What made you do such a thing in the first place?" Beverly asked.

Harriet sighed. "All my life I have wanted to go on the stage. I tried every way I knew to get a part—especially in *Angels Arise*. I didn't mean to keep up the pretense very long, just until Beverly or Shirley introduced me to some producers and I got a part. Then I was going to tell you the whole story. I didn't think it would really hurt anyone."

"Tell me," Beverly asked, "how did you happen to know about my Cousin Harriet?"

"When I was a runner-up in the Miss New York contest last year, a publicity agent became interested in promoting me for the stage. He arranged a trip abroad, for the usual build-up. While we were in London, I met your Cousin Harriet at a tea. When she learned that I was from New York and was interested in the stage, she asked me if I had met you, the famous author of *Angels Arise,* and then remarked that you two had never met. The publicity man immediately cooked up this stunt."

"It seems such a silly way to go about—"

"My agent assured me that when the newspapers finally got the story the publicity would be a big boost for me," Harriet returned. "When I agreed to do it I had no money, no job—I was discouraged. I was willing to do anything. The chance for nice clothes and an opportunity to get into the theater seemed like heaven."

"But why me?" Beverly demanded. "There are lots of playwrights—more famous ones."

"It would have been too hard to do with a really famous one," Harriet said candidly. "And besides, I had dreamed of playing in *Angels Arise*. Maybe it was foolish, but I didn't care much about any of the other plays."

The three Alpha Delta girls were silent. What could they say? Each of them recognized the sincerity in Harriet's voice. They believed that her ambition and desire had been thwarted to the point where she was willing to grasp at the faintest hope to realize her dream. No matter how strange her actions might seem to them, the girls were aware that desperation could drive anyone to great lengths.

Lenora drew a deep breath and it seemed to break the spell that had held them.

"What would you like me to do?" Harriet asked quietly. "I promise never to bother you again."

"I know what it means to want a part in a play," Shirley said, remembering the days she had tried to find her place. "I—I'll need an understudy next season. It isn't much but—"

"I'd love it," Harriet said in a faint voice. "I—I—can't say thank you—" her voice thickened and tears started to her eyes. In another moment she had turned and fled out the door.

The three girls remaining looked at each other in thoughtful silence.

"Somebody say something," Lenora urged.

"Have you ever wanted anything that badly?" Beverly murmured. "So badly you would have done anything to get it?"

"It is like living on a merry-go-round," Shirley began smilingly. "The strangest things happen to us!"

Her statement was to find even further fulfillment in Beverly Gray's Challenge as we follow the girls on their vacation and find them involved in new adventures.

THE BEVERLY GRAY

MYSTERY STORIES